Roudybush, Alexandra
Blood ties

BLOOD TIES

By Alexandra Roudybush

BLOOD TIES
FEMALE OF THE SPECIES
SUDDENLY, IN PARIS
A GASTRONOMIC MURDER
A SYBARITIC DEATH
A CAPITAL CRIME
DEATH OF A MORAL PERSON
BEFORE THE BALL WAS OVER
THE HOUSE OF THE CAT

BLOOD TIES

ALEXANDRA ROUDYBUSH

PUBLISHED FOR THE CRIME CLUB BY

DOUBLEDAY & COMPANY, INC.

GARDEN CITY, NEW YORK

1981

All of the characters in this book
are fictitious, and any resemblance
to actual persons, living or dead,
is purely coincidental.

First Edition

ISBN: 0-385-17339-3
Library of Congress Catalog Card Number 80–1852

Printed in the United States of America

For Katherine Wheaton, with grateful thanks

BLOOD TIES

PROLOGUE

When Sarah Dessein died in a fire in her home, the facts elicited at the inquest were straightforward and the coroner did not hesitate to categorize her death as an unfortunate accident, taking the opportunity to animadvert at some length on the folly of smoking in bed.

Her husband, Carl, on the witness stand, looked like a man on the verge of collapse. His face was pale, dark circles under reddened eyes testified to sleepless nights, his hands shook, and his voice, as he gave his evidence, was barely audible. His wife, he testified, telephoned him to say that she was working late and would not be home to dinner. Mr. Dessein therefore decided to go out for a snack. When he arrived home shortly after ten o'clock, Sarah's car was not in the garage so he assumed she had not yet returned. Passing from the garage into the kitchen, he noticed a smell of burning. When he opened the door into the hall and found it full of smoke, he retreated to the kitchen and called the fire department.

"Your wife's room is on the second floor?" the coroner asked.

"Yes."

"But you didn't go up?"

"It never—" His voice broke and his shoulders shook with noiseless sobs. Finally he managed to control himself enough to answer. "It never occurred to me that she could possibly be home," he cried.

By the time the firemen found her, Sarah was quite dead. Cigarettes, matches and what was left of a whiskey-and-soda were on the little table by the bed; a cigarette was found, half burned, deep in the mattress.

Sarah Dessein, on the death of her first husband, Manny Stein, had inherited 51 per cent of the shares of Moses & Stein, popularly known as M & S, a Southern California men's clothing chain. When the business was started shortly after World War I, Californians, while they dressed more casually than men in other parts of the United States, still wore suits and, as it was generally acknowledged that one got good value at M & S, the chain prospered over the years. The hippie-flower-children movement of the sixties, however, was disastrous for conventional haberdashers, particularly in California, and the firm's profits plummeted. Isidore Moses, who had succeeded Manny Stein as president of the firm, suffered a stroke and died and Sarah had to take over; under her direction, the red ink gradually turned black. Ruthlessly, she closed down unprofitable outlets, redecorated and hired young buyers. M & S began to provide the sort of garments youth (and, soon, older men in search of youth) wanted.

Sarah's marriage to Carl Dessein was, on the whole, considered a sound and sensible move. Carl had been with the firm from the time he left high school, starting in the workshop as a general dogsbody and rising to the position of cutter while studying accountancy at night school.

World War II, which he spent uneventfully in the Quartermaster General's office, briefly interrupted his career, but after demobilization he returned to M & S as a junior bookkeeper. At the time of his marriage to Sarah, he was the manager of one of the firm's most important branches. If he was disappointed not to be advanced to an executive management position in the central office, he concealed it admirably. Moreover, he was not too surprised; M & S was very much a family firm and most of the executives were assorted members of the Stein & Moses clans; he knew that Abe Stein, Sarah's teen-age son, would eventually succeed his mother.

The marriage was a shock to thirteen-year-old Abie, who, after his father's death, had enjoyed his mother's undivided attention and had come to think of himself as the man of the family. While he and his stepfather seemed to get along well enough when they were together in public, the boy began to spend more and more time away from home; on two occasions he ran away. Sarah knew, however, that adolescents whose parents remarried invariably went through a difficult period of adjustment and she decided to send the boy to boarding school in the East. On his return, she hoped, he would be ready to make friends with his stepfather and they could all live harmoniously together.

As it turned out, that never happened. When his mother threatened to cut off his allowance if he didn't return home to attend U.C.L.A., Abie got himself a job as a "runner" for a firm in the garment industry on Seventh Avenue and attended New York University at night. Pushing racks of clothes through the streets all day and studying at night began to pall, and Abie was about to give in to his mother's repeated requests when the Korean fracas escalated into war. He joined the Marines and, after training, had ten days' leave before shipping out. Those ten days convinced him that he could never tolerate his stepfather. It was while he was in Korea that his mother died.

Although her death was front-page news in Southern California newspapers, it was of regional interest only. Abie could not have known of it in any event because he was, at the time it occurred, a prisoner in North Korea; it wasn't until the hostilities were over that he learned he was an orphan.

When Abie was flown back to California Jake Cohen, the attorney for Moses & Stein as well as for the Stein family, went to visit him at the Veterans Administration facility where he was recuperating.

"God! You're a bag of bones!" the lawyer exclaimed when he saw the exhausted, gaunt man he had known as a cheerful, robust boy.

"You should have seen me a month ago," Abie said. "I scared myself when I looked into the mirror. A Korean prison camp isn't exactly a health resort. But I survived, so I was luckier than most."

"Well, '*dulce et decorum est pro patria mori*'!" the lawyer said, with a grin.

"Yeah, but I'm Ashkenazi on my father's side and

Sephardi on my mother's and that doesn't add up to Korean."

"When are they going to let you out of here?"

"Maybe at the end of next month."

"What are your plans?"

"There's only one plan. I'm going to get out of the Marines as fast as I can. Who's running the business now that Mom's gone? Who owns it?"

"Why, naturally you own it. At least, you own the controlling interest, in accordance with your father's will."

"I thought he left everything to Mother."

"Everything was left to her during her lifetime," the lawyer corrected. "On her death, however, it all reverts to you."

Abe Stein was silent for a moment.

"What about C.D.? Is he running things?"

"You mean Dessein?"

"Yeah. What did he inherit?"

"Sarah named him beneficiary of her life insurance policy. Outside of that, he inherited nothing—not even the house, which, as you may remember, actually belongs to your cousin, Paul Moses. Your mother rented it from him."

Abie gave a sigh.

"Gee, that's a relief. I've had nightmares about his having taken over M & S."

"There was never any question of that."

"Is he still running the Vine Street branch?"

"No. He quit M & S altogether after Sarah's death. I'm not sure he's even in California. We all felt very sorry for him when she died; I don't know that I've ever seen a man more broken up."

There was a silence.

"Rubbish!" Abie finally spat out. "C.D. didn't give a hoot in hell about Mom."

The lawyer smiled paternally.

"Abie, you weren't at the inquest; his hands shook and he could hardly talk. Sarah's death was a terrible blow to him. I know how you feel about him. But you have to admit you were kind of difficult for a while; C.D. didn't have it too easy with you."

"You don't have to weep for C.D. I can tell you one thing for sure; it wasn't Mom he was interested in, it was *me*."

"You?"

"Yes, me. I was unbelievably naïve at the time, even for thirteen, and it took me a while to catch on. I only thought it was funny that he came into the bathroom so often when I was taking a shower; after a while I always locked myself in. It wasn't until he removed the lock that I began to get the glimmer of an idea of what this was all about. That's when I ran away the first time."

"Abie! You should have told somebody!"

"Who? Even though I was a kid, I realized I couldn't tell Mom."

Jake Cohen looked troubled.

"You're sure? You didn't just misunderstand?"

"I'm sure. I once had to kick him in the groin to get his hands off me. How much did Mom's insurance come to, by the way?"

"Two hundred and fifty thousand."

Abie gave a whistle of surprise.

"And they were only married about five years—that's fifty thousand bucks a year. Not bad! In fact, it's so good it makes me wonder."

"Wonder about what?"

"Mom's death. Was there an autopsy?"

"No. The coroner seemed to feel that it was all quite straightforward. You've seen the newspaper clippings I saved for you, haven't you?"

"I skimmed them. Now I'm going to reread those clippings very, very carefully."

"Why?"

"Well, for one thing, Mother didn't smoke. She couldn't; she was allergic to tobacco. If she tried to smoke a cigarette, she'd get a terrible asthma attack and you'd think she was going to pass out."

"But wouldn't Carl have known that?"

"Very possibly not. Mother didn't believe much in doctors for herself, though she always called one if Father or I had anything wrong. But she thought that the body, if left alone, took care of itself, so she never talked about any health problems she had. She just accepted the fact that she couldn't smoke and left it at that. I don't think she cared much. As a matter of fact, she didn't drink, either, but there was no physical reason for her not to and she could have started drinking to keep Dessein company. But the combination of the two worries me very, very much. I suppose C.D. arranged for her cremation?"

"Yes, but she asked to be cremated in her will."

"What luck for him," Abe said bitterly. "I suppose there's nothing we can do?"

"I can't think of anything," the lawyer answered after a few minutes' reflection.

"When I get out of this dump I'd certainly like a few minutes alone with C.D. I want him to explain to *me* what happened to Mom."

"It won't bring your mother back."

"Maybe not, but I'd enjoy giving that bastard a hiding. I learned a lot about how it's done while I was a prisoner: I'll have the marks till I die and I'd feel better if C.D. had some, too."

"Forget it; breaking up Dessein won't get you anything except a pack of trouble. 'Vengeance is mine, saith the Lord.'"

"I'll share it with him," Abe said, with a tired smile.

CHAPTER 1

The most important thing Felicia Wenham and Hilary Tarrant had in common was considerable wealth. They also shared a grandfather, William Makepeace Kincaid, inventor of the Kincaid Calculator, which was the source of that wealth. Regretting, as so many had before him, that his days on earth were numbered and that he could do little to control the fortune he had amassed after this mortal coil had been shuffled off, Mr. Kincaid was nonetheless determined to do the best he could to prevent his two daughters from squandering the money he would leave them. After poring over lawbooks and consulting experts, he set up trusts that were such convoluted marvels of legal ingenuity that they were later used in law schools as examples of how far it was possible to negate the generally accepted principle that the hand from the grave should have but limited control over the destinies of the living.

Even before their father's death, each of his daughters, when she reached the age of eighteen, received a five-figure tax-free income which increased in geometric progression as she got older. These trusts were managed by a law firm which prospered mightily even though the Kincaid trust was its sole client.

Louise, the elder of the two beautiful Kincaid sisters,

married suitably and with all the requisite fanfare John Archibald Wenham III, a good-looking young man of impeccable lineage, kindhearted, irresponsible and lazy, who had succeeded, with some difficulty, in obtaining a law degree and passing his bar exams. He hung out his shingle but his office was little used except as a refuge when he wanted to get away from home. He had trouble keeping a secretary since the girls he hired complained that working for him was like being condemned to forty hours a week of solitary confinement.

Louise, inheriting her father's Presbyterian work ethic and embarrassed by a husband who was perfectly content to live on unearned increment, tried to spur John Wenham to greater professional efforts. But she merely made him feel so guilty about the difference in their respective incomes that, like many of his drinking companions in the mid-twenties, he began to play the stock market with a small inheritance from his mother. The success of some initial speculations encouraged him to increase them; then came the 1929 crash and he was wiped out financially.

Louise and John Wenham begat Felicia.

Elizabeth, the younger sister, upset family tradition by eloping with Godfrey Tarrant, a Hollywood cameraman. Godfrey had no money but he had a dream, which he succeeded in communicating to his wife. Relieved by the income from the Kincaid fortune, of the responsibility of providing for a family, the two of them proceeded to make the dream come true. Buying some secondhand equipment, they set off for Persia to film the first of Tarrant's Historical Travelogues. The early years were barren (except for the birth of their daughter Hilary); then, suddenly, there was a demand for the travelogues, not only from movie theaters but from schools and colleges, first in English-speaking countries and then from all over the world, as teachers discovered this painless method of instructing the young in ancient history. Ultimately, Tarrant's Travelogues generated income, even after expenses, that exceeded their income from the Kincaid trusts.

The modesty of the travelogues' beginnings contributed in no small measure to their success. Since Godfrey could not afford to pay actors or build scenery for his films, the work was done on location, using native actors. The method was simple: the Tarrants would choose an event in history, say, the battle of Thermopylae. They would spend about a month on research, then go to Thermopylae for the filming. Their most successful production was a film of the career of Alexander the Great in six episodes. The Tarrants adored their work and had a good time doing it.

Hilary was born in California and was left in her aunt Louise's care, seeing her parents only briefly and rarely. After her third birthday, however, she accompanied them on their travels and was only returned to her aunt when their wanderings took them to corners of the globe which even they who believed that children who were loved could adapt to almost any kind of life considered unsuitable. By the time Hilary was seventeen, she had gone to local schools in India, Greece, Persia, Afghanistan, Turkey and Egypt and knew Urdu, Arabic, Greek, Turkish,

Farsi and Pushtu. This glorious life came to an end when her parents were killed in a plane crash in the Indus valley. When Hilary went back to her aunt's house in California she was, in effect, returning to the only home she had ever known.

Hilary and Felicia had got along well enough together as children. Hilary, although she was two years younger than her cousin, laid down the rules of the games they played, decided which movie they would go to see and, in general, was the leader. Felicia didn't mind; she seemed to like having someone else make decisions for her.

But Hilary had been eleven at the time of her last stay in California and was seventeen when she returned in 1936. In the six intervening years there had been changes in California, not the least of which was her aunt's divorce from Felicia's father, whom Hilary had liked, and her remarriage to Gerald McDougal, a wealthy insurance broker who believed in General Motors, General Foods, General Electric, the Republican Party and God in that order. The house in Pasadena had been sold and the family had moved to the more opulent McDougal estate in Bel Air.

After two years of desultory study, Felicia had dropped out of college and filled her days with Junior League activities, luncheons with friends, and tennis and swimming parties. She was also, when Hilary returned to the United States, dutifully falling in with her mother's rather elaborate plans for her debut.

"To tell the truth, I dread it," she said one day, examining her face in the mirror in Hilary's room. "I wake up in a sweat from a nightmare in which I'm one of those girls behind whose backs boys wave a five-dollar bill to get cut in on."

Hilary came over and stood beside her cousin.

"That's ridiculous! Admittedly neither of us has a face to launch a thousand ships, but who wants to?" Hilary began to laugh. "To tell the truth, nobody, looking at us, would guess that our mothers were famous beauties! These things certainly skip a generation. We'll probably be wildly jealous of our beautiful daughters. But if you're scared about this debut, and I can't blame you, just tell Aunt Louise that you don't want one."

Felicia sighed.

"I can't do that. Anyway, Mother may be right and a debut *is* the nicest way to meet boys of your own class when you're a newcomer to a community."

"You've been here ever since Aunt Louise married Gerald more than three years ago; you're not exactly a newcomer."

"I was at school in Switzerland during two of those years. At any rate, I don't know any boys."

Her cousin looked at her in amazement.

"You can meet them other ways. Are you planning to sit on your duff waiting for a knight on a white charger? Get a job! If it's men you're after, you'll find them at work."

"I don't know how to do anything except speak fairly good French," Felicia answered dispiritedly.

"You're only nineteen! Learn how to do something."

"What?"

"Well, that depends. What would you like to do?"

Felicia shook her head.

"I can't think of anything."

"Oh, you're hopeless. Why don't you go to Maine and talk to your father?"

"It would make Mother mad; she'd feel I was disloyal."

"Felicia, show some guts! You've got a right to talk to your father."

"Yes, of course. But it wouldn't be worth the trouble. If someone disappoints Mother, she kind of likes to sweep it all under the rug. . . . She pretends he no longer exists. I don't dare even mention him."

"How on earth did your father disappoint Aunt Louise? He was a very nice man."

"He wasn't a very successful one. He didn't care about corporations and businesses and, in law, that's what brings in the dough."

"I love the idea of your mother worrying about money. I know exactly how much her income is because I've inherited *my* mother's share, which was the same as Aunt Louise's. If there's one thing you and I are alike in it's that neither of us is on the way to the poorhouse."

"You're rich, but I only get what Mother gives me. If I wanted to marry someone she disapproved of, she wouldn't let me have a penny."

"That's true right now. But you'll be getting your own share of the trust when you're twenty-one and then you can marry anyone you like."

"I don't want to be married for my money!"

"Well, nobody does. But money can be very useful to a young couple when the husband is just starting a career. Look at my parents! Dad would never have made the success he did of the travelogues if Mother hadn't had the money to subsidize those first trips. The fact that she had the energy and talent to be a marvelous photographer was less important than the fact that she could pay for cameras and equipment."

"Mother was telling me this morning that you've decided to go to England in September. She's quite unhappy about it," Felicia said, changing the subject.

"Yes, she and I had pretty much of a knock-down and drag-out last night. But she can't stop my going if the trustees are willing. I don't see why she wants to. There's nothing wrong with being a nurse, though I know that to her it's only one step above being a maid."

"She doesn't understand why you don't take your training here instead of England."

"I explained it all to her. You become a nurse in three years in England and it takes at least four here. It might even take me longer because I've never been to school except in places like Greece and India and Persia and the American education system is diploma-mad. She says that I'm too young to be 'alone' in England, but I won't be 'alone.' Dad was a Scot and, even though Aunt Louise disapproves of them (mostly because they raise sheep) I've got relatives scattered all over Britain. I want to get the training over, and then I'll start thinking about what I really want to do. It'll probably be archaeology. I knew lots of archaeologists when I was traveling with Father and Mother and they seem to lead fascinating lives."

Felicia looked at her cousin in surprise.

"But you've just said you're going to become a nurse!"

"Father's theory was that everybody should have some skill, no matter how humble. We talked about it often and I promised that if anything ever happened to him, I'd learn to do something which would keep me from starving."

Felicia looked nonplussed.

"Neither of us is in any danger of dying of starvation."

"There's always the possibility of war, revolution, or other disasters which could wipe out your fortune. Look at the Russians who had to leave their country after the Communists took over, and the people who lost all their money when the stock market crashed, and those who have to get out of Germany now—to mention only examples in our lifetime. So Father thought everybody should be able to be self-supporting. Trained nurses are in demand everywhere. Good cooks, of course, are, too, and, since I like messing around in a kitchen, I thought of going to a cooking school—maybe the Cordon Bleu in Paris. But I'm really not much interested in pandering to spoiled palates. Perhaps it's because I've lived in parts of the world where the major preoccupation of most people was getting enough to eat that three-star restaurants shock me, even though I enjoy eating in them." Hilary sighed. "It's awfully hard to live up to one's own principles, isn't it?"

CHAPTER 2

Hilary Tarrant entered St. George's Hospital in London in 1936 and it took every ounce of willpower she had not to walk out again.

I don't know whether I'll ever make it as a nurse [she wrote to Felicia], but I'll be worth my weight in gold as a cleaning woman. All I do is scrub, mostly unpleasant objects with hard-to-get-at corners. I wish someone would redesign bedpans, for instance.

When mother read your last letter she wanted to cable you to give up that horrid nursing business and come home. But I pointed out to her that you were as obstinate as a mule and that her cable would be the surest way of making you stay on at St. George's [Felicia answered]. For once she agreed I was probably right.

I *guess* I'm having a good enough time right now. My debutante days are about over but I still get invited to a lot of parties. Mother insisted on my having a Christmas dance so I did and, of course, all the boys had to dance with me because I was the hostess. I don't have a real beau, though. The trouble is that rich boys can marry any pretty girl they like so they're not interested in me. And when poor boys give me a rush, I always feel it's my money they're after.

Your letters make me wish I could do something, too, though nursing doesn't sound very tempting. I wanted to go to secretarial school but Mother put a damper on that, pointing out that I couldn't spell, among other things.

Love,
Felicia

"This time next week where shall I be?
Not in this academy.
No more dirty bread and butter,
No more water from the gutter.
No more spiders in my bath,
Trying hard to make me laugh.
If old matron interferes,
Knock her down and box her ears.
If she doesn't care for that,
Rub her face in fish's fat," [began Hilary's final letter from St. George's]. I don't know what "fish's fat" is unless it's the oil from smoked salmon and there are much nicer things to do with smoked salmon than rub matron's face in it.

I'm overtired and run down—these last months have been hellish—and I'm going to spend the summer on my cousin Peter Tarrant's farm in Scotland. He has sheep, cows and children and says he and his wife could do with a little help with the latter. I've never had much to do with kids so it should be interesting for all of us. Tell Auntie I'll probably come home in September to see about taking some courses in archaeology at U.C.L.A. Of course, there's a good deal of talk of war right now, but I don't suppose it will come to anything.

Hilary Tarrant kept her promise to her father and finished her training at St. George's Hospital, in time to join the FANY as an army nurse when World War II broke out in September of 1939.

"I was so happy when I'd finished my training," Hilary wrote to Felicia. "Now, of course, I'm stuck with it. I'm 20, healthy and a British subject, though I *feel* American. But I wouldn't be able to live with myself if I skipped back to safety in the U.S. now. And Father used to say that one should always welcome any new experience, as it's bound to be interesting even if it's disagreeable. He was right about so many things he was probably right about that; I'll soon know whether war is interesting or not."

As it turned out, the first two years of the war Hilary found thoroughly dull. She was stationed in military hospitals in Great Britain but, except for a flurry of activity at the time of Dunkirk, they were overstaffed and she missed the hurly-burly of St. George's. She found the rigid discipline, the monotony of routine tasks, and the total absence of intellectual stimulus hard to endure. So it was with pleasure that she learned of her transfer to Cairo.

At first, Cairo also proved to be a disappointment.

Hilary's activities were still circumscribed by army regulations and rules of conduct both written and unwritten; travel around Egypt was impossible and she was reprimanded for having been seen sitting in a coffeehouse with an Egyptian who had been a friend of her father's. There was, however, plenty of social life.

"If it's men you want," Hilary wrote to her cousin, "this is where you should be. Even pudding-faced girls find themselves courted. *You'd* be ten deep in beaux."

But Felicia, for the first time in her life, had struck out on her own and was working in a defense plant in Seattle. And she had acquired a beau about whom her mother knew nothing.

While Hilary had her share of admirers, none of them really interested her until her meeting with Captain Ian Maitland. Their encounter took place in a secondhand bookshop.

"Here, I'll get it for you," a pleasant baritone voice said behind her as she stood on tiptoe to try to take down a book just out of her reach. "Which one is it you want?"

"That one, if you don't mind," Hilary said, pointing.

A hand stretched out from behind her and took the book from the shelf.

"Here you are."

Hilary turned to look up into the serious gray eyes of an exceptionally handsome, slender young man.

"It's in Arabic," he said, blowing the dust off before handing the book to her.

"Yes. It's the Koran," Hilary answered as she turned the pages. "I've been trying to find an illuminated one. This has some illustrations but they're not very good. Still, the printing is clear and relatively easy to read. I think I'll buy it."

"I had a great-aunt once who, whenever she had a problem, used to open her Bible at random to find a solution," the young man said. "It wasn't quite as 'at random' as she pretended; she knew her Bible well enough to be able to avoid bits which would have made sibylline interpretations impossible. Oddly enough, sometimes the answers were surprisingly apposite. Do you suppose that would work with the Koran?"

"Probably as well as it does with the Bible."

"Let's try."

"What question do we want answered?"

"We could ask what the war has in store for us. Close the book and then I'll open it somewhere near the middle."

This was done.

"Well, what does it say?"

" 'The Greeks have been defeated close'—no—'nearby,' " Hilary translated slowly. " 'But soon they will be victorious, for this is the will of Allah.' " Hilary looked up and laughed. "It's certainly relevant! Of course, the defeat of the Greeks the other day is hardly surprising. But let's hope the prophecy that they'll soon be victorious is true."

"You really do know Arabic."

"Was that exercise just to check on whether I did or not?"

"Frankly, yes. How do you know the language so well?"

"One learns it at school."

"Does one indeed! I must have gone to the wrong schools. You know, you sound more like an American than an Englishwoman—yet you're wearing our uniform."

"My mother was American, my father British. I don't have any very intense feelings of belonging to either country. Until I went into nursing in London, I'd never lived in England at all and not very much in the United States, though I do seem to think of it as 'home.'"

"Where actually did you live?"

"The Near and Middle East, Persia, Greece, Turkey, Afghanistan, India." As Hilary looked up into the serious gray eyes, she wondered who he was. There was something familiar about him, yet it was hard to believe she could have forgotten him if she'd ever met him; he was quite the handsomest man she had ever seen off the screen. The screen! That rang a bell. A movie she had seen just before the war . . .

"Did you once play in a picture called *The Yellow Ticket?*" she asked. "The leading actor looked very much like you; he had a beautiful voice, too, like yours."

"Thank you. I wish it had been. But it was Laurence Olivier. The resemblance has been mentioned to me several times and I am always flattered. My name is Ian Maitland and I'm no thespian. How about having a drink with me?"

"I'm Hilary Tarrant," she answered, glancing at her watch. "I'm afraid I can't take you up on your invitation today," she added regretfully. "I have to be on duty in about an hour and Matron's the rigid sort. She'll have my hide if I'm late."

"I'll walk to the hospital with you if I may; I'd like to know more about you. Were your parents missionaries?" Captain Maitland asked, falling into step beside Hilary.

"Heavens, no! Poor Father . . . definitely not the missionary type."

"Was he a diplomat?"

"No indeed. And now you've had your two guesses."

"Oh, but one always gets three before the king says 'Off with his head.' "

"Then we'd better stop at two. It seems hardly worth losing your head!" Hilary laughed. "Anyway, this is the nurses' entrance."

"When can I see you again?"

"Next month, perhaps. I'm on night duty for the rest of this one."

Captain Maitland frowned.

"Oh, I can't wait that long," he said. "What about nine o'clock tomorrow morning?"

"Don't be ridiculous!" Hilary exclaimed. "I'll have just gone to bed at that time."

"I think you're forgetting yourself, Lieutenant Tarrant," Ian Maitland said, grinning down at her. "You don't tell your superior officer he's 'ridiculous.' "

"I keep forgetting," Hilary said impatiently. "I've never read the King's Regulations; anyway, we're certainly not in the same *branch* of the Army."

"What branch do you think I'm in?"

Hilary looked over the various insignia on Ian Maitland's uniform. "I suppose I should be able to tell. But I'm afraid the best I can do is recognize that you're a captain. So, good night, sir," and Hilary saluted smartly before going through the hospital gate.

An abortive raid on Crete a couple of days earlier had resulted in heavy casualties and the wounded men began to be carried into the hospital shortly after Hilary went on duty. So she spent the night in the operating theater as surgeons worked on the wounded. Since the hospital was short-handed, she kept on working even after her relief came on and it was nearly ten o'clock when the last man was taken down to a ward.

Hilary was aching with fatigue as she removed her operating gown and pinned on her cap. She was standing in the corridor trying to decide whether to have some breakfast or to go straight to bed when an orderly approached.

"Matron wants to see you," he said. "I was to watch out for you and tell you as soon as you came out of the theater."

"Oh, dear! What on earth could I have done?" Hilary exclaimed. "I'd better go and tidy up; I'm a mess."

"She said you was to go at once."

The matron of the military hospital in Cairo was a formidable woman, six feet tall, who was invariably referred to behind her back by both staff and patients as the Cuirassier. Her ancestors had fought in every English war since Sir Geraint Hellier won his spurs at Agincourt, and it was a brave man who failed to cringe when the Honorable Honoria Hellier was on the warpath. Yet when one of her young nurses had to undergo a serious operation, she had been too upset to assist the surgeons and had stood outside, wringing her hands while tears poured down her cheeks.

"You're late," the matron said when Hilary knocked and came in.

"Yes. I've just left the operating theater. The men who were wounded in the raid on Khania were brought in last night."

"Do you think I don't know what goes on in my own hospital?"

"I spoke without thinking," Hilary said with a smile. "I'm absolutely certain you're aware of *everything* that goes on in your hospital."

The matron looked mollified.

"You'd better go to bed right away. However, please arrange to be called by two o'clock at the latest. Orders have come through that you are to report to SOE at three o'clock."

Hilary looked baffled.

"SOE?" Hilary echoed.

"You must have heard of Special Operations Executive," Matron said impatiently.

"I'm afraid I haven't," Hilary said.

"It was Special Operations that organized the commando raid on Khania."

"Oh. Well, what has SOE to do with me?"

"My guess would be that they want to recruit you."

"Recruit *me?*"

"This echoing habit you have is very irritating."

"You mean I wouldn't be a nurse anymore?"

"Surely that wouldn't upset you. I never had the impression that you cared much about nursing."

Hilary felt herself turning red and, tired as she was, couldn't prevent tears from rising to her eyes.

"I see," she said, trying to keep her voice from trembling. "I had not realized my work was unsatisfactory."

"Silly child! You're one of my best nurses; I always feel I can rely utterly both on your skill and on your common sense. But the fact is that you nurse entirely with your head and not with your heart. Am I wrong?"

Hilary sighed.

"I'm afraid you're quite right. But in time of war so many people have to do things they don't in the least like doing. I'm fortunate in having a useful skill."

"I understand SOE is under the impression that you have other skills which are rarer than nursing and which will be of greater use. That is why I must lose you to them, assuming you agree to join the organization."

"That would depend. I certainly don't want to sit in an office doing translations all day long, if that's what they have in mind. That's my idea of hell. I may not be mad about nursing, but it certainly beats pencil-pushing."

"I don't believe they do much 'pencil-pushing' here in Cairo," the matron said drily. "Now get some sleep, then report to SOE. Ask for Major Small. That will be all."

Major Small reminded Hilary of one of the lawyers who handed the Kincaid trusts. He was a short, stocky man with thick, silver-rimmed glasses, heavy jowls, and a potbelly. Hilary was disappointed; she had expected someone more romantic. But she warmed to the little man when she noticed that the blue eyes behind the bifocals were both shrewd and humorous.

"Captain Maitland seems to think we will be very fortunate if we can persuade you to join us."

"Was it Captain Maitland who suggested me? I only met him once—yesterday—and had no idea what he did in Cairo."

"He's my assistant. He tells me you speak several languages, including Arabic, fluently. What are these languages?"

"The two languages I know best are Greek and Arabic. But I also know some Turkish, Urdu, Pushtu and Persian. I traveled with my parents in the Near and Middle East from the time I was three."

"What did your father do?"

"He filmed travelogues."

"Tarrant's Historical Travelogues! Of course. What an interesting life your father had! It's tragic that it was cut short so suddenly." He paused. "Well, how do you feel about joining the Firm, as we call it?"

"I'd like to know a little more about it," Hilary said cautiously.

"Yes, of course. First of all, I should make it clear that you cannot be conscripted into SOE. If you join us, it will be entirely of your own volition. Also, you are completely free to leave whenever you wish to or to refuse any mission."

"What sort of work would it be? I should tell you that I don't at all care for office work and I particularly detest doing translations."

"There will be none of that, though you may be required to act as an interpreter occasionally," Major Small replied with an amused smile. "You may well end by longing for the quiet comfort of an office," he went on. "I won't hide the fact that the jobs we send our people on can be very dangerous; some involve parachuting into enemy territory.

"And there is one other important consideration you must bear in mind," he said. "If you're caught, the *best* that can happen to you is that you'll be shot or hanged."

"Thank you for warning me," Hilary said. "I'll certainly bear that comforting thought in mind. I suppose rape and torture are the other alternatives."

"Two of the others," said the major.

"Is there anything else I need to know?"

"Just one question. Do you have any personal objections to killing?"

"I don't think so," Hilary said reflectively. "It would, of course, depend on circumstances. I killed a man once when I was about thirteen and remorse never really kept me awake nights."

"You killed a man?"

"It was self-defense. When my parents and I were living in Azerbaijan, just outside Tabriz, I drove Mother into town in our trap. It was during Ramadan and on my way home I passed a procession of Shiites covered with blood, flogging themselves, in a state of exalted religious frenzy. I was fairly tall for my age and the sight of an unveiled woman, driving a horse, infuriated them and they began to throw stones at me. Well, I'd seen a woman stoned to death once and it had been, to put it mildly, unpleasant, and I had no desire to share her fate. So, when one of these men reached up to catch my horse's bridle, I made him rear and then crash down with his forelegs on the man's head. The only thing that bothered me was the squishing noise the wheels made going over the man as we galloped on. It taught me one thing: that bravery is not particularly admirable. It's merely a normal reaction to danger—much like eating when one is hungry. Does that answer your question?"

"It does," Major Small said gravely. He picked up the phone. "Ask Captain Maitland to come in, please."

"If I decided to join you, and you decided to have me, what would happen next?" Hilary asked, as they waited.

"You would be sent to England for training."

"How long would that take?"

"Several months—not less than three. We have several centers, each with its specialty; as soon as you finish one course, you'll be sent to another."

"What would I learn?"

"Many things you never expected to have to know, from parachute jumping to silent killing."

"Good afternoon, Ian," Major Small said as Captain Maitland came in. "I've just had a most interesting talk with your protégée and I hope she'll agree to join the Firm. What I'd like you to do now is arrange language tests."

Hilary felt herself blush when the major referred to her as Captain Maitland's "protégée" and her heart, normally a well-regulated muscle, skipped a beat as he smiled down at her. But before they could speak, they were interrupted by a voice over the intercom.

"I'm sorry to interrupt you, sir, but Communications

has succeeded in contacting Colonel Myers in Greece and he is anxious to talk to you and Captain Maitland. He urgently needs instructions from London."

"Tell Communications we're on our way," Major Small answered.

"Yes, sir."

"I hope you don't mind waiting; we probably won't be long. We've been trying to get in touch with Colonel Myers for several days and were getting worried," Major Small said and the two men hurried from the room.

Hilary wandered over to the window and as she stared out she debated what answer to give Major Small. Suddenly, as she thought over her recent conversation, the lines of ragged laundry hanging out to dry in the filthy, sunless courtyard disappeared and she and her father were riding from Peshawar back to a camp in northern India. She could hear the enthusiasm in her father's voice as he talked about Alexander of Macedonia. "And he'd conquered what he thought was the world by the time he was thirty-two, overcoming all obstacles and achieving a fame that has never been surpassed in all the centuries since his death. He never was afraid to take chances. He's a perfect example for all of us. We are awake so little on this earth that we must make the most of every minute. Never be afraid of danger. *Live*, my darling girl, while you can. You'll be dead a long, long time."

Hilary was still standing by the window when Major Small returned alone.

"Have you come to a decision? Or would you like a few days to think things over?"

"That won't be necessary, sir," Hilary said. "If you still

want me after you've checked up on me, I'll be glad to join you."

"Don't make any hasty decisions you'll regret," the major warned.

"I've always found that one doesn't really make decisions; life makes them and you go along. This is no exception."

"Darling Felicia," Hilary wrote hastily the night before she was due to leave Cairo. "Delighted to hear about your new role of 'Rosie the Riveter.'

"Don't worry if you don't hear from me for a while. I'm being transferred to another branch of the Army and shan't be able to write. But all's well."

And so Hilary Tarrant began her connection with British Intelligence, a connection that was to go on intermittently for more than thirty years. And her friendship with Ian Maitland was a lifelong one.

CHAPTER 3

Hilary's training began in a school on the outskirts of the New Forest and she found the work so excruciatingly boring she almost requested a return to nursing. Here she underwent hours of physical training, which she had always hated. She also learned to identify planes and to recognize regimental insignia and badges of rank and branches of service both of allies and of the enemy.

More interesting work followed. She rather enjoyed the training in industrial sabotage and was interested in learning about explosives and how to manufacture them with readily available materials.

"It'll be handy if I decide to become a burglar after the war is over," she said to Ian Maitland over lunch one day when their leaves in London happened to coincide. "In fact, a lot of things I'm learning will come in handy if I decide to take up a life of crime."

It was in a school on a loch in the Western Highlands that the training was the most exhausting. For three weeks she hardly slept. Carrying a gun and a fifty-pound rucksack and guided only by a compass, she tramped up and down the countryside, through fogs, thick mists and rain, tripping over obstacles invisible in the dark, falling into gullies and sliding down hills. Nor could she count on rest at the end of the day. All too often, hardly had her head touched the pillow than she was shaken awake and ordered out again, this time in battle dress, equipped with a balaclava helmet, a tommy gun, grenades and explosive charges, a fighting knife, a clasp knife, a pair of wire cutters, a torch and emergency rations and wearing felt-soled boots. During these night exercises she crawled, often in the rain, on her stomach, trying not to make a sound.

It was here, too, that Hilary became thoroughly competent with guns and where she learned to assemble and dismantle a Bren gun with remarkable speed. Her nurse's training came in handy when she was instructed in the art of silent killing; it was easier for her than for her fellow trainees, all men, to find the vital spots in which to sink the knife for the quickest lethal effect.

"For someone as small and delicate-looking as you, I'm surprised at how well you've done," the doctor in charge said. "You're in perfect health, too. Not the slightest trace of overfatigue, yet goodness knows, you trainees have been getting little enough sleep."

"It's a very deep sleep when we do get it," Hilary said. "And I think perhaps my size is a help: I don't have much weight to carry around. I'm like the Highlanders, small and wiry."

But it was the last part of her training that Hilary dreaded—the parachute jumping. At first, she was dropped through the hole in the fuselage of a dummy plane to learn the correct position for leaving the aircraft. But Hilary tossed and turned in an agony of dread the night before her first scheduled jump. When the time came, Hilary and five other students were fitted with heavy parachutes and straggled out to the airfield.

It's certainly true that misery loves company, she said to herself as she noted that her companions were all a greeny-white color.

The six climbed up into the belly of the plane near the tail and, following the instructions of the sergeant, sat around the exit hatch in dropping order. To her horror, Hilary found herself number one.

"It's better to be the first," one of the others consoled her. "It cuts the agony of waiting."

"I read somewhere when I was a kid that parachuting wasn't anything you could practice; you had to do it perfectly the first time," another man said.

"Cut the gab and listen to me," the sergeant said as he clipped the static lines to a wire along the fuselage just beneath the roof. "As soon as the red light goes on for action stations, I'll call your number and raise my hand. You swing your legs over the hatch. When the light turns green, I'll drop my hand, shout 'Go!' and you jump. Don't look at the lights; just watch my hand. And for Christ's sake, don't freeze up on me. You're jumping from a thousand feet, so you'll get a punch from the slipstream. Don't forget—body stiff, knees and feet together, hands pressed close to the sides, and look up as you leave the aircraft, but as soon as the chute opens, keep your eyes on the ground all the way down. And land easy, rolling on your side."

The hatch was opened, the cold poured in and the sudden roar of the engines was deafening. Barely conscious,

Hilary heard the sergeant's shout of "action stations number one" and saw his hand go up. She forced herself to throw her legs over the edge of the hatch.

"Go!" the sergeant cried, lowering his hand.

With a yelp of terror, Hilary leaped into the void, remembering to look up until she felt a violent pull under her armpits as the parachute opened.

Suddenly everything was all right, and as she floated gently down to earth in silence, Hilary felt almost giddy with pleasure. Following instructions, she stiffened her body as though standing at attention in the air, then she was careful to keep her eyes on the ground, which seemed to be moving up to meet her. She rolled as she landed, suffering no greater damage than a scraped knee, and she could hardly wait to go up again. Hilary had become a parachutist.

When she had completed her training, she reported back to Cairo as being available for assignment. For some time she did little but act as interpreter at SOE interrogations and spent most of her free time sightseeing, with Ian Maitland when he was free or alone. Then she was given an assignment that delighted her.

Turkey, neutral during World War II, was wooed by both the Axis and the Allies, so that the British Government was delighted to comply with a request from the Turkish Government to give technical advice on establishing a hospital by Lake Van, not far from the Persian border. The building had been completed and Hilary was assigned the task of ordering the necessary equipment and organizing the day-to-day operations of the hospital. This gave her some months of work she thoroughly enjoyed and also enabled her to improve her Turkish, which had become rusty.

I feel like Florence Nightingale in Scutari [she wrote Felicia], except that I don't have to bother about patients, as we don't have any yet. I guess I'm like those people who love being professors so long as they don't have to give classes and have plenty of time to do research and write books at someone else's expense.

Do tell more about what you're doing in Seattle—I'm so glad you finally got off on your own.

Love, Hilary

P.S. By the way, did I tell you I saw your father before I left London? He's with OSS and having a thundering good time. He took me to dinner at the Savoy. Do write to him! He'd love to hear from you.

It was while Hilary was still in Turkey that she received an ecstatic letter from her cousin.

I'm in love! His name is Walter Simmons and he's in officer training school studying to be a gunnery officer. I met him at a USO dance ten days ago and he's taken me out every night. He doesn't have much money, of course. Last night he took me to a chess club, of all things, and we played classical records while he taught me chess moves. He won't let me pay for a thing, not even a bus ride. And, oh, Hilary, it's *me* he likes; he doesn't know anything about my money. I'm so happy I can hardly bear it.

Naturally, I've kept all this a secret from Mother—I don't want her to spoil it, so for goodness sakes don't mention it to her.

Walter hasn't asked me to marry him yet, but I think he will. Oh, I do hope everything is going to work out!

Love from Felicia

When Hilary finally left Lake Van, she was given three weeks' leave and took the opportunity to fly back to California to attend to some business and visit her aunt and Felicia, now Mrs. Walter Simmons.

CHAPTER 4

Felicia's first marriage took place in 1942 after a courtship of the type that is generally characterized as a whirlwind one. A month to the day after she met Walter Simmons, Felicia married him, having notified her mother of the wedding twenty-four hours before it took place. In spite of Mrs. McDougal's almost hysterical pleadings to postpone it, Felicia stood firm.

"Walt's had his orders and is shipping out next week," she said. "So it's got to be now."

"Just wait till he comes back," her mother begged.

"How do I know he's coming back?" Felicia asked. "A lot don't, you know."

"At least come home to get married. We can arrange a nice wedding at St. Peter's and Gerald can give you away."

"It's going to be a civil wedding before a justice of the peace," Felicia said. "If I had anyone give me away it would be my father and he's in England."

"How do you know that?" her mother asked, momentarily diverted from the subject at hand.

"I got a letter from Hilary. She's seen quite a lot of him, she says. He's with the OSS."

"Old fool! Going to war at his age!" Mrs. McDougal fumed.

"Mother, he's only forty-five! Anyway, to get back to my wedding, if you want to come, I'd love it. But I don't want Walt—" Felicia stopped suddenly.

"You don't want Walt what?"

"I don't want him to know we're rich," Felicia blurted out. "Not until after we're married. I don't think it's occurred to him that I might be well off. And I want it to stay that way. So if you're coming, don't come in the Cadillac," Felicia added.

"What about his education? His people?" Mrs. McDougal wailed. But her daughter had hung up.

Mrs. McDougal was, on the whole, not too displeased with her son-in-law. He was a nice-looking young man with a pleasant manner and had attended a good private school in Washington where his father was fairly high up in the civil service. It could have been much worse. Walter had been at college at the time of Pearl Harbor and had at once joined the Navy. All in all, Mrs. McDougal was fairly content. One thing, however, did disturb her slightly and that was the difference in their ages: the bride was four years older than her new husband.

Felicia was wildly happy. And her marriage was something she had achieved for herself, without her mother's assistance.

After her husband had shipped out, Felicia found she was pregnant. So, pressed by her mother, she had given up her job and gone back to Bel Air to await her child's birth and her husband's return. Her brief spurt of self-reliance was over.

Walter Simmons, Jr., was eight months old when Hilary came back to California for a brief visit.

"You know, he looks just like your father," Hilary said when her cousin proudly brought him forth.

"Don't let Mother hear you say that. She says he's the image of the Kincaids."

"Time will tell. And you're looking wonderful, Lisha. Motherhood agrees with you."

"Oh, it's marvelous! If only Walter were here! He hasn't even seen his son yet. Of course, I've sent him scads of photographs, but Junior changes so every day. It's almost unbelievable."

"What's Walt going to do when the war is over?"

"He wanted to go to Cornell to become a vet but Mother has other ideas. She wants him to go to Harvard Law and says she'll buy us a house in Cambridge and give us an allowance while Walt studies for his degree."

"Oh, Felicia, no!" Hilary exclaimed.

"What's the matter?"

"If Walt wants to be a vet, let him be one. The most important thing in life is for a man to enjoy his work. He can get away from his parents, he can divorce a wife and, if he wants to, sire a second batch of children if the first lot is unsatisfactory. But he's stuck with his career and he'd damn well better like it. It makes all the difference between leading a relatively happy life or, to quote Thoreau, what most men lead, one of 'quiet desperation.' "

"But he might like being a lawyer."

"What you mean is that it's more socially acceptable. Well, it's your life." Hilary shrugged.

"Tell me about you, Hilary. Your life must be awfully exciting."

"Not exciting, exactly. Disrupted and sometimes

difficult. By the way, what about the clothes I left here when I went to England? Did Aunt Louise throw them away? You can't get anything without coupons now and it would be quite a windfall if my old things were still around."

"You know perfectly well that Mother never throws anything away. She has all your things stored in the attic in labeled packages and garment bags. I wouldn't think you'd need ordinary clothes much, though. Don't you have to wear uniforms? And do you like nursing any better now?"

"It has its moments."

For the first few days, Hilary did little but eat and sleep. It was bliss to be able to go to bed knowing she would not have to get up till morning and equally blissful to sit down to chilled honeydew melon, or freshly squeezed orange juice, to eggs whose immediate provenance was the shell rather than the tin, to crisp, lace-edged corn cakes, oozing butter and dripping syrup.

"You're skin and bones, child," Mrs. McDougal said as she pressed food on her niece.

"Not really, Auntie. There's not much surplus fat (though there will be if I go on like this), but there's a good deal of muscle. I'm really very fit right now."

Just then Felicia, who had been upstairs bathing her baby, rushed into the room.

"Walt's here!" she exclaimed breathlessly. "He just called from the airport. Hilary, be an angel and finish dressing Junior while I get the car out. Walt's actually here! I'm so glad you'll get to see him before you have to go back overseas! I'll meet you in the garage," she called as she hurried off.

Hilary found Walter Simmons a pleasant enough young man without much personality. She was willing to believe that he had married Felicia in ignorance of the fact that her family was wealthy, but she suspected, from his obvious efforts to please Mrs. McDougal, that he was now determined to benefit from the situation.

He stayed at his mother-in-law's for a couple of days, then the three of them flew to Washington to visit his parents.

"How do you like Walter?" Mrs. McDougal asked after the young couple had gone.

"I didn't really get to know him," Hilary said cautiously. "He seems very pleasant. Anyway, Felicia seems happy with him and that's the important thing."

"Yes, but will she stay happy?" Mrs. McDougal asked, lighting a cigarette. "I wish he were a little more *solid*."

"Oh, Aunt Louise! Does anybody *stay* happy? The most we can hope for is having our periods of unhappiness and happiness more or less balance out. Anyway, the literature of the world is filled with attempts to define 'happiness'. Dryden calls it 'rest from pain,' which, I think, is as close as you can get."

"I want more than 'rest from pain' for my child and I'll do everything I can to arrange it."

"Auntie, there is one thing I do know: happiness has to come from within and cannot be 'arranged' by someone else."

"I can at least help with his career; I'll send him to Harvard Law School when he gets out of the service."

"Don't you think it would be better to let him do what he wants to do, which, according to Felicia, is to become a veterinarian?"

"Well, I'm not going to have Felicia married to a veterinarian."

"Why not? There are few phonies among vets, and you can't say that about lawyers—or doctors, for that matter."

"Really, Hilary! Fortunately, Walter is being very sensible. We had a long talk last night and he agrees that Harvard Law would be the place for him. Of course, he'll be older than a lot of his classmates but he's still young and there's no rush."

"Yes, he is young. It bothers me a bit. Felicia *looks* sensible and adult, but in spite of their difference in years, I think she's even more immature than Walter."

"That's good. She'll let herself be led by him."

"Why on earth should she be led by anybody? It seems to me she has reached the age to make her own decisions. I think one trouble with her is that you've always dominated her."

"I've always done what's best for Felicia!"

"What you thought was best for her, which is quite a different thing. Now I'm afraid she'll always look for some stout oak around which to wrap her tendrils. And, Walter doesn't strike me as being exactly a stout oak; he's more like a rather weak reed which won't offer much purchase for clinging."

"We'll see how things work out," Mrs. McDougal said with a sigh. "Legal training is important because it offers you an entry into several profitable and interesting careers."

"I think it's more important to like what you do. Look at Felicia's father: he told me once that he had never wanted to be a lawyer but his father pushed him into law.

He had wanted to be a marine biologist. By the way, where is Uncle John now? You know I saw him in England?"

"I have no idea and care less," she said shortly. "About you, now. You're going back to London?"

"London first, then Cairo."

There was a lengthy silence.

"There is something I think I should tell you, Aunt Louise. When I report back next week, it will be to another branch of the service where my superiors feel I'll be more useful."

"I should have thought that in time of war nobody could be more useful than a nurse," Mrs. McDougal said.

"That's true in a way. But nurses can be trained in a comparatively short time. It's the education I got traveling around with mother and father that's apparently more interesting to the powers that be."

"That surprises me. You never *had* any education worthy of the name, Hilary. I wrote to your mother time and again begging her to send you to us so that you could go to a decent place with girls of your own class instead of those dirty village schools. Why, you were never even taught to speak French: all you learned were a lot of useless languages."

"You're quite wrong; I had an *excellent* education. Every single day, including Sundays, I had two solid hours of study in English, history, literature, Latin and mathematics. And as for my languages, it's because of them that I'm going to be able to get away from bedpans."

"If you remember, I never thought much of your idea

of becoming a nurse in the first place," Mrs. McDougal said with a sniff. "What are you going to be doing now?"

"I'm not supposed to tell anybody, but, since you and Felicia are about all the family I have, I believe I will. Don't repeat this to anyone, and that includes Felicia. I've been transferred to intelligence work. My job in Turkey was pretty straight, though I kept my eyes and ears open and made some contacts which may come in handy."

"I guessed as much when you were talking about your languages being useful. I take it you mean you're going to be a spy?"

"It sounds a bit melodramatic, doesn't it?" Hilary said. "To tell the truth, I don't know in just what branch of Intelligence they intend to use me. The wonderful thing about being in the military is that you don't have to do any thinking or make any decisions. It's all done for you. Now I must go, Auntie. I have an appointment at three-thirty with old man Chadworth. I know the money from the trust, if I suddenly die, will go to you and Felicia automatically, but I feel I should make a will to cover what Father left; royalties are still coming in from the travelogues. Incidentally, they are expected to bring in a good deal of money if television develops the way it is expected to after the war. Is it okay if I name you as coexecutor? I'm leaving the non-Kincaid money to a children's hospital run by nuns in Calcutta. You and Felicia have all you need and more."

"Is there much?"

"Quite a bit, actually. I've spent hardly anything for the past four years, so it's accumulated. There must be about three million dollars now."

"As much as that? To think that we thought your mother was throwing herself away on a fortune-hunting wastrel! Well, do what you think best, my dear. I'll be glad to be an executor but pray it won't be necessary."

Two days later Hilary flew back to Cairo—ten months after she had first left. Her heart gave a little lurch as she saw Ian Maitland waiting at the arrival gate.

No man has a right to be so handsome; it's just not fair, she said to herself and she smiled as she walked toward him. But there was no answering smile, although he returned her smart salute.

"So you made it back," was his only greeting as he led the way to the car, and he didn't speak as they were driven into the city. Mindful of the fact that he was now her commanding officer, Hilary, too, was silent; she wondered what had brought about the change in him. She also noticed that he now wore the insignia of a major but made no comment on his promotion.

"You'll be staying here at our hostel until we've arranged for your drop," he finally said, rousing himself from his abstraction as the car stopped. "The driver will take your bag in and tell them you've arrived. Then we'll go on to the Mustam Building. You'll come back here later."

"Yes, sir," Hilary replied. If he could be curt, so could she.

He preceded her into his office, sat down at his desk, motioning her to a chair, and picked up the phone.

"I don't want to be interrupted," he said and Hilary saw that he looked tired. There was a long silence and it was finally Hilary who broke it.

"Is something the matter?" she asked. "Did I flunk?"

"No, no! Quite the contrary. You did exceptionally well. Everyone was very pleased with you. And the Turkish government has expressed their appreciation."

"I'm glad," Hilary said. She looked at him inquiringly.

"We have an assignment for you," he said curtly. "Rather a dangerous one. Please don't think it's my idea; I argued against sending you but was overruled. If you feel you'd rather not take it on, tell me now."

"Please go on," Hilary replied, her green eyes hard.

"The mission will involve your being parachuted into Greece. In about ten days. We just have time to provide you with an identity and a cover story, and rehearse you in it, as well as with documents and suitable clothes. All right?"

Hilary sighed.

"All right, except I wish it were sooner. I've always hated waiting; it gives one too much time to think."

Major Maitland rose to his feet. "Come on, we'll go to see Major Tuff and his people; they'll explain what they want you to do for us."

A plane which was to bear Hilary, weapons and ammunition, clothes and shoes, medicines, mail, and gold to pay the guerrillas—all to be parachuted into the mountainous region of Thessaly where a British mission was hiding out—was scheduled to leave Cairo on a moonless night. Hilary had been given some pills and instructed to go to bed early the night before her jump and had conscientiously done so but found it impossible to rest and was relieved when Ian Maitland telephoned her.

"Are you all right?" he asked.

"A bit jittery and I'm certainly not going to be able to sleep."

"How would you like to come to my place? We can have a little supper and then listen to some Mozart, which is very soothing, and I have a pretty good collection of the concertos."

"I'd love that."

"I'll pick you up in ten minutes."

Hilary had not been exposed to much music in her life and an evening of Mozart was something of a revelation to her.

She woke up the next morning, rested and refreshed, to find Ian gone. There was a note pinned on the pillow beside her.

"You're to be at the airport by noon and I'm sending a car to fetch you. Chin up and God bless!" she read.

That night she left on her assignment.

CHAPTER 5

The deep animus that Abe Stein felt toward the man who had been his stepfather did not diminish with the passage of time. Quite the contrary: his long convalescence gave him plenty of time to brood, and he planned to track down Carl Dessein as soon as he was strong enough.

It was by accident, however, that he found him. One of his mother's last innovations at M & S before her death was the establishment of a rental department at the main store in Los Angeles. It was here that Abe began his training.

"I'm going to leave you in charge this afternoon," Bob Jacobson, the manager of the department said to Abe. "I'm going to the dentist straight from lunch and then I'm going home. It shouldn't be a particularly busy afternoon. I got a call from Jack van der Alst. His twin sister is getting married tonight and Jack is going to give her away, since they're orphans. Jack is six feet five and I've hung the only garment we have that might be big enough for him in fitting room number four."

"So Moira's getting married, is she? I went to school with Jack van der Alst. I'd have thought, with all those millions his father made from mustard before he drank himself to death, that Jack could afford to have a suit made to order."

"They only decided to get married three days ago," Mr. Jacobson said as he put on his coat.

"Poor Moira is a good scout, but she's over six feet tall and homely as the proverbial mud fence, so I suppose when a prospective bridegroom loomed on the horizon, *carpe diem* became her motto before he had a chance to recover his eyesight."

"Perhaps it was the glitter of gold that blinded him," Jacobson replied as he left.

Abe was helping a pianist select tails for his concert that evening, when he felt something heavy strike him on the back.

"Abraham Lincoln Stein," Jack van der Alst exclaimed, "what are you doing in this dive?"

Abe summoned a salesman and joined his old classmate.

"It's good to see you," he said as he ushered him into Mr. Jacobson's office. "I hear you're marrying off Moira tonight."

"I sure am. Never thought I'd live to see the day! Not that Moira isn't a great girl—too great, in fact. There's so much meat around her heart of gold that no one suspects it's there."

"We've got a suit put aside for you to try. Let's go in the fitting room. Who's the lucky man?"

"You wouldn't know him. Guy by the name of Dessein, Carl Dessein."

Abe stopped in his tracks and stared up at the young giant beside him.

"Carl Dessein?" he repeated.

"Yeah. Do you know him?"

"Yes," Abe finally answered dully. "Yes, I do know him."

"Moira's damn lucky, don't you think? He's a good-looking one if you go for the Cary Grant type. And he oozes charm."

Abe remained silent, unsure of what to do.

"Listen," he suddenly said. "I'm going to take you out and buy you lots of strong black coffee. I want to talk to you and I want you sober."

"I like that! I'm not drunk! Not at this hour, at least. And the wedding is in a few hours and I've got to rent that suit!"

"Never mind about the suit. If you still want it after you've heard what I have to say, we'll come back here and I'll give you the damn thing. But if you've got any sense, you won't be needing it."

Abe Stein was right. The marriage between Moira van der Alst and Carl Dessein did not take place.

CHAPTER 6

When Hilary found herself in the plane from which she was to parachute into Greece, she was so sure she was living a dream that she was not afraid. It was this conviction that she was asleep and would shortly wake up in her bed that enabled her to carry out her orders.

"Those must be the identification fires," the pilot called out. "Better get set."

"There are only two fires, sir," the sergeant observed. "According to instructions, there were to be three, in the form of a triangle."

"Hell! I think you're right. We'll try the next valley." The plane climbed once more and veered to the right. "There they are—three of them," the pilot exclaimed as he began to lose altitude again. "Get ready to parachute the loads down. We'll make sure they have time to reach the ground before the body jumps; she won't want to be hit on the head by a box of shoes. Okay?"

Hilary, still in her dream, watched as case after case was thrown out of the plane, which then rose to circle once more around the signaling fires. On command, she moved over to the open hatch, dangling her legs in the void, and, like an automaton, jumped when the sergeant gave the signal. It was only as she was floating down toward the ground that she suddenly realized that this was no dream, that the earth coming up to meet her was the soil of Greece. There were several men grouped around one of the fires, looking upward; two were wearing British uniforms. This heartened her, and when one of the officers waved to her, she waved back. She landed without a scratch and, as she lay on the ground, looked up at the bearded face of an officer bending over her.

"I'm Major Singer," he said. "You all right?"

"I'm fine, sir," Hilary answered as she struggled out of the parachute and got to her feet.

"In that case, let's get away fast. Somebody may spot the fires and come to investigate."

As Hilary was helped out of her parachute harness and her jump suit, the cases that had preceded her out of the plane were picked up by the guerrillas, the fires were doused and the party moved off silently, with Major Singer and Hilary bringing up the rear.

"We've got quite a long walk ahead of us over rough terrain. Not too tired?" he asked in a low voice.

"Not at all," Hilary whispered back.

After about an hour's march, Major Singer called a halt and, walking to the head of the column, spoke to the other uniformed officer. After conferring briefly, the two men came back to Hilary.

"This is Captain Sampson," the major said. "He's going on with the others but you and I and Spiros here"—and he gestured toward a heavily armed bearded guerrilla standing beside him, who grinned and bobbed his head at Hilary—"are going to spend what's left of the night with one of Spiros' sisters, who lives nearby. All right, Peter, off you go. I'll join you at Solinos as soon as I can. If they didn't forget to send us the whiskey, be sure to leave some for me."

A five-minute walk brought Hilary and the two men to what seemed to be an abandoned farmhouse, but as soon as Spiros gave a distinctive whistle, the door was opened. It wasn't until Hilary and her companions were inside and the door was closed that a candle was lighted, revealing a bare room furnished with a rough wooden table and two chairs.

"Do you want something to eat?" Major Singer asked.

Hilary shook her head.

"In that case, we'd better get whatever sleep we can; we've only got a couple of hours. Spiros and I'll doss down here while you and Maria take the other room."

Hilary spent what was left of the night on the floor next to Maria, rolled up in a blanket.

Hilary and Major Singer sat over a breakfast of bread and barley soup for a long time while the officer explained her mission to her. "No wonder Ian was appalled," she thought to herself, but all she said was: "You're sure this von Rabenstein is in Dhomios."

"He was there yesterday. And no more repair work on the Asopus viaduct can be done until some parts are received from Germany; we and the EAM guerrillas are going to do our best to keep those parts from getting through. You should have at least a week or ten days to see what you can do."

Hilary ate a mouthful of bread.

"You mean, to seduce von Rabenstein," she said drily.

"That seems to be what it amounts to," Major Singer answered, shrugging. "Are you willing to try?"

"I don't seem to have much choice, do I? I'm willing to try but, of course, I can't guarantee success. I may simply not be the type to arouse any of his baser instincts."

"We've been told he is *very* susceptible."

"Why did he pick a little hole like Dhomios for his headquarters?"

"I told you his mother was Greek. That's where she came from and his grandfather, who is in his eighties, still lives there. Dhomios is very pro-German and he feels safe there. Spiros and his younger sister, Anna Giloulianis, whose husband runs the taverna, are the only anti-Axis people in the village."

"I see. Now would you mind going over the whole thing once more, telling me exactly what I have to do *should* I succeed in my Lorelei role."

Major Singer, leaning over the table, talked earnestly for nearly an hour while Hilary concentrated on committing what he was telling her to memory, occasionally interrupting with a question.

"I think that about covers it," the major finally said, getting up. "It's time you and Spiros were on your way. You want to get there early to begin your work for Spiros' sister and her husband at the taverna before the German officers billeted there are up."

"Is von Rabenstein billeted there too?"

"No. He stays with his grandfather, who has the only bathroom in Dhomios. But he joins his fellow-officers for most of his meals. Now you'd better go and change. Maria has some clothes for you, and she'll hide your uniform till you need it again. You know, of course, what it means if you're caught out of uniform?"

"Oh yes. I know. I was told the least that could happen to me would be to be hanged or shot. And I was given a pill to take in case I was threatened with torture. I understand it works very quickly."

When Hilary came back, she was wearing a shabby black cotton dress and sandals. Her hair, drawn back tightly, hung in a long thick braid down her back. She looked very young.

Major Singer smiled a little sadly as he looked her over.

"I have a daughter," he said. "I should be glad she is only fourteen. I hope your father never finds out about all this."

"He's dead," Hilary answered. "And if he's in heaven, he can get some guardian angels busy on my behalf. Shall we go?"

Hilary's first two days at the taverna were spent cheerfully fending off the attentions of Colonel von Rabenstein's fellow-officers. The colonel himself, however, had not yet made an appearance at the inn and, knowing how little time she had, Hilary was becoming anxious. She was relieved to learn from Spiros that Germany's railroad engineering genius had flown to Belgrade to attend a meeting with Marshal von Weichs and was due back the next day. When she finally saw her prey, she was surprised. He was a slender young man with blond hair and long-lashed deep blue eyes; nothing like the monocled Prussian martinet she had conjured in her mind's eye. He seemed much too young for his rank.

She made no attempt to attract his notice as she went about, serving food and drinks while laughingly repulsing the advances of the others. All the officers in Dhomios, as

Hilary knew from the black epaulets, collar patches, and piping along the seams of their trousers or breeches, were members of the *pioniertruppe,* or engineers.

As she was hurrying past von Rabenstein's table, carrying a tray piled high with plates, a captain who had been particularly pressing in his attentions to her caught at her braid and jerked her back, causing several of the plates to slip off the tray and smash on the stone floor.

Anna Giloulianis rushed out of the kitchen and, seeing what had happened, slapped Hilary and screamed that she would have to pay for the damage. Hilary began to cry as she knelt down to pick up the fragments of plates, and von Rabenstein took the innkeeper's wife aside.

"Don't scold her," he said, pressing money into her hand. "It wasn't her fault." Hilary went back to the kitchen with the rest of her dirty plates, leaving the officers laughing and talking. She seemed to be the subject of their badinage and she very much regretted her ignorance of German. When Anna, who did understand the language, came back into the kitchen, she motioned Hilary to accompany her to the cellar, where most of their confidential talks took place.

"You won't have any trouble," Anna whispered to her as they filled a wicker basket with bottles of wine. "They are laying bets on how long it will take von Rabenstein to succeed with you—without rape."

"I see," Hilary replied thoughtfully. "I shall have to be very careful."

She played her fish skillfully for three days, spending a good deal of what little free time she had with the young

German, but only during the day. Under other conditions she thought she probably would have enjoyed the engineer's company, but her fear of inadvertently making some remark out of keeping with her role of a fifteen-year-old Greek orphan, daughter of a country schoolteacher, made their conversations rather one-sided. Hilary's participation consisted chiefly in putting in an innocuous question from time to time.

"I shall have to leave you soon," von Rabenstein said one day as they walked beside the stream that meandered through the village. "Will you miss me?"

Hilary nodded, giving her companion what she hoped was a shy, encouraging glance.

"Let's go off by ourselves tomorrow," Anatol murmured, putting his arm around her shoulder. "I know a lovely place in the woods where we can have a picnic and go swimming. There is a pretty little mountain lake, surrounded by pine trees and we'll be quite alone."

"I'll have to ask Anna. I can only come if she allows it."

"She'll allow it if I speak to her," Anatol replied. "I can hardly wait until tomorrow!" And he began to kiss her urgently.

But Hilary broke free.

"It isn't tomorrow yet," she said with a provocative smile as she sped away.

When Hilary returned to the taverna, she slipped up to the attic, where she had a cot. Here she lay, sickened by the part she was being forced to play and longing to be a thousand miles away. The knowledge that she was in a trap as lethal as the one she was setting for Anatol von

Rabenstein brought the realization that there was nothing she could do but go on. "It's my life against his," she said to herself, "and I don't want to die yet if I don't have to."

There was a scratching at the door and Anna Giloulianis came into the room.

"He talked to me about a picnic," she said. "So it's to be tomorrow?"

"Yes, tomorrow. Tell Spiros and explain to him where these woods are so he can make arrangements with Major Singer. I don't know when von Rabenstein intends to leave—probably around eleven o'clock. I hope they all get there in plenty of time!"

"I hope so too. You're not giving them much notice."

"When he made the suggestion, it seemed to me the best thing to do was to agree, rather than to try to postpone it; he told me he was planning to leave soon, so I suppose the parts he was waiting for have arrived or are about to. Oh God! How I wish this were all over!"

When Anatol and Hilary met the next morning, the German was dressed in shorts, a tee shirt and sandals, the first time she had seen him out of uniform; he seemed more like a student than a thirty-two-year-old railroad engineer.

After a long, hot uphill climb over a rocky trail the pine woods seemed deliciously cool. Hilary gave an exclamation of pleasure when she saw the trees reflected in the clear water of the mountain lake.

"It looks marvelous," she said. "I'm so hot the water will sizzle when I get in." She went behind a bush to take off her dress; under it she wore a bathing garment she had fashioned from an old dress she'd found in the Giloulianis attic. Anatol, who had stripped, laughed when he saw her.

He swam to where she stood poised on the edge of the water. He reached out to grab her but she eluded him by diving into the tarn over his head, then not surfacing until she reached the other side. By swimming vigorously, Hilary succeeded for a while in keeping out of Anatol's grasp, but the mountain water was icy and she realized she would soon have to leave the protection of the water.

As she hoisted herself out, she listened for the sound of Major Singer and his men but, except for the chirp of crickets, the woods were silent. Anatol was out of the water and beside her as she got to her feet.

He took her in his arms and pressed his lips on hers. Still holding her tight with one arm, he tore her bathing dress off, then carried her over to a blanket he had spread out over the pine needles.

After a last, despairing look around for the help that should not have been far away, Hilary sighed and surrendered to Anatol's urgent lovemaking. It was nearly an hour before he finally fell asleep, one arm over her body. The sound of men's voices roused him and he sat up to find himself surrounded by armed bearded guerrillas, led by a uniformed British officer. Hilary, now dressed, stood among them. She had successfully concluded her mission.

For Hilary, it turned out to have been easier to get into Greece than to leave it, and it was two months after the accomplishment of her assignment that radio orders were received from SOE Cairo. Captain Sampson, one of the radio operators, and Hilary were to set out on what turned out to be a nightmare trek in weather that became bitterly cold over rugged portions of arid, inhospitable mountains, their only food what they could steal—their skill and training in "silent killing" was used on any livestock they happened to find—their uniforms in rags, their shoes tied on with sacking and string. The trip also took a great deal longer than had been allowed for by officialdom in Cairo. When the three of them finally reached the designated meeting place, they found that the submarine had given them up and left.

The radio equipment no longer functioned and, to cap it all, Hilary became sick. She begged the others to leave her but they turned a deaf ear; they carried her into a mountain cave and did their best to feed and care for her, but for nearly a week she was severely ill. Aided by her own medical knowledge, she began to recover; the three of them held a council of war and decided that the only chance of survival seemed to lie in stealing a boat and setting out to sea, hoping to be picked up by some British or other friendly craft. Of course, if they were picked up by Germans, that was another story, but there was a slim chance that their uniforms would ensure them prisoner-of-war status.

On the fourth night at sea the radio operator, crazed by thirst, jumped overboard; Hilary, in high fever, became delirious and lost consciousness. She didn't recover it till she found herself in a hospital, Ian Maitland standing beside her bed. She never had the slightest recollection of their rescue, and months passed before she recovered physically from her experience. It was during this time that Mrs. McDougal, advised of her niece's serious condition by Hilary's superiors, flew across the Atlantic to be with her.

Hilary emerged from her experience much changed. While she had been gay and full of life, she was now silent and withdrawn, accepting any assignment she was given without comment and performing it superlatively. When she was told she had been awarded a medal for her work, she refused it. She prepared an official report on her mission as soon as she was well enough, but after that she never spoke to anyone, not even to Ian Maitland, about what had happened.

CHAPTER 7

Felicia's marriage to Walter Simmons had begun to disintegrate when they were living in Cambridge and Walter was attending Harvard Law School. They had had their third child, Timothy, and Mrs. McDougal had bought the young couple a large Colonial house; she and Felicia had spent an enjoyable couple of months in the pursuit of authentic early-American antiques. After Mrs. McDougal had returned to California, Felicia continued on her shopping spree.

Walter seemed restless and discontented and was not doing too well in his studies. Also, the young couple was lonely. This was due partly to the fact that most of Walter's classmates were going to school on G.I. funds, in many cases assisted by their wives' jobs. Even those with wealthy parents maintained a simple life-style, whereas Walter and Felicia employed a married couple as well as the children's nurse who had come with them from California, paid for by Mrs. McDougal; this intimidated the other young people.

Walter began skipping classes, and Felicia, going over the statement of their joint account, was distressed to find that Walter was writing a good many checks without letting her know, which confused the bookkeeping. When these were returned from the bank, she saw they were mostly made out to "cash." When she tried to question him about these sums, he stormed out of the house in a rage, sometimes not returning till the following day.

The definitive break came when some checks of hers were returned from the bank marked "insufficient funds." Such a thing had never happened to her before and she thought it must be the bank's error until she discovered that a few days earlier Walter had bought two cars for himself, one of which was a Cadillac.

A telephone call to her mother brought Mrs. McDougal on the scene and she at once decreed a divorce. The two cars were returned to the dealers, Walter was ordered out of the house, which was placed, furnished, on the market, and a month later Felicia, the children, Myfanwy Evans, their nanny, and Mrs. McDougal were on their way back to California.

For a time after her divorce, Felicia lived quietly with her children in her mother's house, a careful, conscientious, though rather remote parent. As far as Walter, Jacqueline and Timothy were concerned, they might never have had a father. Mrs. McDougal issued the fiat, and Felicia assented to it, that all recollection of Walter Simmons should be expunged: his clothes, books, pipes, school and navy souvenirs, even the Morocco-leather prayer book his mother had given him for his confirmation, were disposed of and, as Myfanwy Evans was warned, Walter Simmons' name was never to be mentioned. One Christmas, when a large box of toys arrived for the children from their paternal grandparents, it was sent back, unopened. Mrs. McDougal was not one to permit herself to recognize her own mistakes. She was subconsciously aware that she was to blame for her daughter's present situation but, unable to admit to the possible fallibility of her judgment, she preferred to bury the mess.

For Felicia, uneventful days succeeded each other. Like her mother, she had her charities and a pleasant social life and she did not lack for would-be suitors. But the failure of her marriage, which had been her one revolutionary act against her mother's dominance, increased her self-doubts and she was rather relieved than otherwise that her prospective beaux tended to be dull, middle-aged, bald and paunchy and, in several cases, overly fond of the bottle. She couldn't help remembering, during some sleepless hours, that Walter had been young, handsome and fun.

Felicia read somewhere that the ideograph for the word *trouble* in Chinese was two women under one roof, and she thought of this when she and her mother were beginning to behave like a married couple moving toward divorce. They could agree about nothing and Felicia, though she sought her mother's advice, then invariably began arguing and complained that she was tired of being ordered around like a child.

Finally they agreed it was time for them to live separately and Felicia bought a house about twenty miles away—near enough to make meetings easy but too far for daily dropping in.

It was at the close of the seventh year after the divorce that Felicia came to know Carl Dessein. Dorothy James, a cousin of her mother's, met him at a supper party and was quite taken with his dark good looks and quiet elegance and somewhat overwhelming charm.

"I must say that it's a nice change to see a well-dressed man these days," Mrs. James said to her husband, as they left the party. "Let's ask him to dinner with Felicia one night soon. He's charming and looks just about the right age."

"Who is he?"

"I think he must be some sort of professor; he mentioned working at Bel Air Institute. He's rented the house next to Marianne's."

"And he works at that two-bit college? Listen, even the president of Bel Air couldn't begin to afford the rent of that house—or of any house in the neighborhood."

"He's probably got private means."

"How come he's not married? Is he a queer?"

"I don't know why you're being so disagreeable about the poor man. I think Marianne said he was a widower."

"Boy! Well, Felicia'd better move fast . . . widowers don't grow on every bush in California."

"I'll ask them to dinner next Friday, when the Paisleys are coming."

The dinner party was a success and Dorothy James was smugly pleased with herself when she saw that Felicia and Carl Dessein seemed to have clicked.

"I heard him ask her to go to the ballet tomorrow night and I was delighted when she said she would."

"Why shouldn't she?"

"Because I happen to know she's supposed to be going

to Joyce Ward's tomorrow. Joyce's husband is out of town so she invited some girls over for bridge, and Felicia is very fussy about keeping her engagements. I really think something may come of this."

"I wouldn't count on it," her husband said as he began to gather up the glasses. "Even the ballet would be an acceptable alternative to an evening of bridge with a bunch of hens."

Shrewd in his judgment of character, Carl Dessein proceeded slowly in his courtship of Felicia and, in the early days, seemed to spend more of his time with her children than he did with her, taking them on picnics, canoeing expeditions and once, when Felicia had been on jury duty, on a camping trip. They were enchanted at finally having a male in their lives, particularly young Walter, and Carl was assiduous in taking him to ball games, in helping him improve his batting skills and his tennis.

The other two were slightly harder to win over completely, though when Carl succeeded in persuading Felicia, who was not partial to animals, to let Jacqueline have a cat and Timothy a dog, they succumbed.

Mrs. McDougal, too, was partial to Carl Dessein, though she questioned her daughter closely about his antecedents.

"Are his parents still alive?"

"I don't think so. He's never mentioned them," Felicia answered.

"Where did his people come from?"

"I've never asked. I believe he did once say that he

came from a French Huguenot family that fled to Switzerland at the time of the revocation of the Edict of Nantes."

"Well, that sounds respectable enough," Mrs. McDougal said somewhat grudgingly. "What's his educational background?"

"U.C.L.A. Then he was at some university in Germany for a while."

"The rent on his house must be high. I shouldn't have thought a bachelor would need a place that big."

"Carl doesn't pay any rent, he just pays for utilities. Marianne Frost has a lot of valuable antiques and, when her husband was transferred to Paris for a couple of years, she went to the institute to see if they could recommend some childless faculty member to house-sit. Carl keeps the place in perfect condition—in fact, he can do anything around the house; plumbing, carpentry, electrical work—he's even a superb cook and keeps Ali Bab's *Gastronomie Pratique* by his bed like a bible."

"Are you going to marry him?"

There was a silence.

"Well?" Mrs. McDougal said impatiently.

"I suppose I will if he asks me," Felicia said slowly.

"You mean he hasn't *asked* you yet? For God's sake, he's been practically *living* here for the past six months!"

"So far he's kind of talked around the question of marriage. But I think he'll propose."

"Will you accept?"

"Probably," Felicia sighed.

"Why the sigh? Don't you want to marry him?"

"In some ways; it'll be wonderful to have someone to lean on, to help me with the children. Walt is getting to be quite a handful; he's been much better since Carl's been around. Yes, I'll marry Carl. I'm tired of being alone."

Dorothy James was ecstatic at the success of her plot and used every opportunity to vaunt the virtues of either whenever she was with the other. But it was to Dorothy's husband, Peter, that Carl talked about the possibility of marrying Felicia.

"I'm crazy about her, of course," he said one afternoon as they sat over a drink after a game of tennis. "But there's one thing that bothers me. The family seems to have loads of money. I've got my job and a bit of money in the bank, but I'm nowhere near Felicia's league."

"Oh, forget that. Dorothy's money comes from the same trust, though she has less than Felicia. There were a lot more children in her branch of the family so the income's considerably diluted. It worried me too at first because I was fresh out of the Army and didn't have a bean when Dorothy and I wanted to get married. But it turned out to be no problem."

"But there is money, then?"

"Ooodles and oodles of it," Peter answered cheerfully.

"And it doesn't bother you to have Dorothy pay for things?"

"Hell, no. I make a good living. We couldn't afford the house we have or the boat or perhaps one of the cars if it weren't for Dorothy. But we wouldn't go hungry if we had to live on what I earn. Stop horsing around, Carl. Felicia's a swell girl. You couldn't do better."

The wedding was a quiet, informal affair at Mrs. McDougal's and Peter James was Carl's best man. The children were excited and pleased; at last they would have a father, like other kids. In fact, everyone seemed content. Only Nanny Evans had her reservations and she kept them to herself.

The newlyweds, after a brief honeymoon, settled down in Felicia's house.

"It's bliss having a husband who has a job," Felicia said to her mother when they were having lunch together one day. "He's out of the house most of the day so it's marvelous when he comes home; we've got something to say to each other."

"Does he ever talk about his first wife?"

"Not anymore. Just after we'd decided to get married, he told me about her. He cried bitterly when he described her death. She had, he said, got in the habit of drinking more and more and he was afraid she might be turning into a lush, which made him very unhappy since he felt he must be to blame somehow. She drank mostly in the evenings and he was careful to check everything before the lights were all turned out to avoid just such an accident."

"Did he inherit anything from her?"

"Next to nothing. It was all left to her son by her first marriage. Carl got a little insurance money."

"Well, that's very sad," Mrs. McDougal said perfunctorily. "Speaking of other things, I got a letter from Hilary this morning."

"Oh, did you? Where is she?"

"The letter was mailed from India but she should be on her way here. She says she's coming via Hong Kong."

"I can't understand what happened; Hilary always used

to write to me regularly. What on earth was she doing in India?"

"Hilary's always wandering around odd parts of the world. The reason for her trip here is that she's started up her father's travelogues again and has to see some radio people in Los Angeles. You wouldn't think she'd go to all that trouble; she certainly doesn't need the money. The last time I saw her was when I flew over when she was so very ill."

"What was wrong with her? You never told me much about that."

"Well, you were having your own problems at the time."

"Was Hilary having problems? I simply can't imagine her ever faced with a situation beyond her ability to cope."

"I guess she coped, all right. When I got there, though, she was very ill; she was delirious and didn't recognize me at first. But, as I told you at the time, she began to get better soon after I arrived."

"Oh, dear, do you suppose it's too late for me to get in touch with her? Carl was saying just the other day that he wants some heavy tussore and she could easily pick it up in Hong Kong since she's coming that way. You can't get it here anymore."

"There's no harm in trying to cable her. I don't have her letter with me but I'll call you as soon as I get home and give you her address there. One of the things she wants to do while she's here is sort out her parents' things, which were left in storage. She's going to get rid of most of the stuff but wanted to know if you or I could store a few things. My attic is so jammed since Aunt Winnie died I simply have no more room. What about you?"

"There's almost nothing in mine. I'll be glad to take her things. Is she staying with you?" Felicia asked.

"No, and it makes me a little mad. She says she can't stand staying with people and insists on going to a hotel. The neighbors are going to think it's very odd—me alone in a large house and my niece staying in a hotel." She glanced at her watch. "I've got to go. Why don't you come over to lunch Sunday? Bring the children."

"We'd love to come, Mother, but I don't know about the children. Carl says that before we were married I was lonely and took them around with me too much. He's probably right that they've become spoiled."

"I don't think they're particularly spoiled; they have exceptionally good manners, though I suppose that's mostly Nanny's doing," Mrs. McDougal said somewhat tactlessly. Felicia flushed a little but said nothing. "I'll expect the two of you, then," and her mother got up to go. "I'll call you as soon as I hear exactly when Hilary is coming."

Abe Stein, not long after his talk with Jack van der Alst, which resulted in the breaking off of the proposed marriage of Jack's sister Moira with Carl Dessein, fell in love, and his courtship of and marriage to Sonia Kramer, a beautiful and talented young harpsichordist, caused recollections of Carl Dessein to dim, along with his hatred. By the time his first two children were born, Abe had all but forgotten Carl Dessein.

Then, one night, looking through the paper while waiting for dinner, Abe's eye was caught by a story on the society page.

"Felicia Wenham Simmons Wed to Carl Dessein" was the headline. Accompanying the story was a photograph of a woman who looked to be in her late thirties. "Felicia Wenham Simmons, daughter of Mrs. Gerald McDougal, of this city, and John Archibald Wenham III, of Boston, was married yesterday to Carl Dessein, son of the late Mr. and Mrs. Charles Louis Dessein of Los Angeles. The wedding took place at the home of the bride's mother, who is the daughter of the late William Makepeace Kincaid, inventor of the Kincaid Calculator. Mr. and Mrs. Dessein will make their home in Bel Air, where Mr. Dessein is connected with the Bel Air Institute."

Just then Sonia came into the room.

"Dinner's ready," she said. "We're starting with a soufflé, so don't dally."

"Say, you've heard me talk about Carl Dessein, my stepfather."

"Yes. The man you thought bumped off your mother."

"Yes. Well, listen to this!" and he read the newspaper piece to her.

"Well, so he got married again," Sonia said. "Surely that was to be expected."

"I suppose. And he's really in the chips this time if that Mrs. Simmons is one of the heirs to the Kincaid fortune. Compared to that, Mother's money was chicken feed."

Abe was unusually silent that evening.

"You know," he said to Sonia as they were going to bed, "I wonder if C.D.'s new wife knows about Mother's death. Do you think I should tell her?"

"No, I certainly *don't.* You can't even be *sure* he killed your mother."

"I'm sure, all right—but I can't prove it," Abe Stein said grimly.

CHAPTER 8

Urged to do so by TV and movie studios and lacking anything else to do, Hilary took over the production of the new Tarrant's Travelogues. For the next few years she spent most of her time traveling. This work also provided a perfect cover for the occasional jobs she continued to perform for the intelligence service.

She didn't return to the United States for a long time, spending as much time as possible in Brittany in an old stone house that was almost indistinguishable from the cliff on which it was perched on a particularly wild stretch of coast. Here she could take long walks, read or spend hours watching the waves crashing against the rocks. Whenever it was possible for him to do so, Ian Maitland joined her there.

A reporter with literary ambitions, on the prowl for a plot for a story, nosed through some recently declassified World War II intelligence archives. He felt he had struck gold when he came upon an account of Hilary's mission to Greece. The resulting novel, *Blood for Drachmas*, became a runaway best seller. Hilary was summering in her Breton home. She had bought the book and, after dinner one evening, began to read it. It wasn't until she had gotten through about thirty pages that she realized what she was reading, and it was dawn before she finished.

The report on which the novel was based was the official one put out by SOE, and by a stroke of luck Hilary's actual name and background were not given. The writer had assumed that Mafina Goulouris, a Greek girl who had died in 1940 in Cairo and whose identity Hilary had been given by SOE, had actually been the protagonist. So, while the background was authentic, the story concerned a superpatriotic Greek girl and her love affair with a Communist guerrilla and was entirely fictitious.

The defenses Hilary had taken such pains to build to blot out the anguish of her Greek experience were swept away as she read *Blood for Drachmas*. The author, she realized, had done his research well: he must have traveled to Greece and interviewed the village folk, and his geography of the village was perfect—the taverna, the public wash house and the bakery were all correctly located, as was the path that led to the tarn and the tall trees where von Rabenstein was hanged. Suddenly Hilary began to cry—sobs she had suppressed for so many years. At first, there had been no time to cry and there was also the fear that if she started she would not be able to stop. Now the storm of tears relieved her and she found she could bear her memories.

The sound of the striking clock reminded her that Ian would be arriving at the airport of Lorient, where she was to meet him. Should she give him *Blood for Drachmas* to read? Suddenly she decided that that was precisely what she would do. It was time that he understood what had motivated actions which must have seemed irrational and incomprehensible to him all these years. Hilary washed her face and drove to the airport and her heart gave its customary lurch at seeing him again after a separation; he had gotten older and his hair was graying but his good looks still moved her as they had since the first time she saw him in the bookstore in Cairo.

The next morning, after breakfast, Hilary handed Ian Maitland *Blood for Drachmas*.

"What's this?" he asked.

"It's a book I want you to read."

He leafed through it.

"Hilary, I never read this sort of thing," he said.

"I'm reasonably sure you'll find it interesting. It's a detailed account of what happened when I parachuted into Greece—straight out of SOE's archives, I would guess. There's a lot that I'm sure even you never knew—and that I had almost forgotten. I want you to read it. You can start right now. I have to drive into Lorient to pick up the lobsters for dinner tonight; I'll get a bite to eat while I'm there and Marie will be here in time to fix your lunch."

When she got home, Ian was still sitting in the library reading, so she made martinis and carried them in. Ian finished the last page of *Blood for Drachmas* as he drank his first cocktail, then shut the book with a snap and put it down on the table beside him.

"Well?" Hilary said.

"How much of this is true? Is this what happened? Did you fall in love with this man?"

"No!" Hilary said explosively, walking to the window that looked out on the rocks below. "Oh, a lot of it's accurate. And the accounts of the destruction of the viaducts at Gorgopotamos and Asopus are very well done. But not what happened afterward."

"Can't you bear to talk about it yet, Hilary?" Ian asked. "It's been so many years. I've always thought it was what made you so brittle . . . so afraid."

"Afraid? It doesn't seem to me that I've been afraid."

"Oh, not afraid of danger—afraid of yourself. Can't you tell me? I don't really know anything except that we hanged von Rabenstein. What was he like?"

"Nothing like the character in this book—not at all the stereotype of the brutal, sadistic Prussian officer this writer makes him out to be." Hilary turned around to face Ian. "He was a gentle, poetic man—an engineer, not a soldier. He loved music; he loved Mozart, Vivaldi, Haydn. He longed for the war to end so that he could go back to his family's business."

"Engineering?"

"Yes. The von Rabensteins built railroads all over the world from the time the steam engine was invented. I never in my wildest dreams thought I could work up an interest in railroad engineering, but Anatol was fascinating when he talked about his work." And Hilary turned back to look at the sea.

"Tell me the end," Ian said gently.

"The end? You know the end: we hanged him. And it was my doing! I trapped him as you'd trap a rat—only to find I'd caught a pussycat." Ian could hear her voice trembling. "When he realized what had happened, he asked to be shot, but Major Singer was afraid the noise of guns might be heard by the Germans, who had patrols out looking for their engineering genius." The trembling voice was becoming choked with tears. "Then he asked if he might be allowed to shave himself before dying . . .

but nobody had a razor." Hilary was now sobbing. "S-s-so he shrugged and walked over toward where the chair was under a tree branch with the rope thrown over it. As he passed me, he saw I was crying and he stopped. 'Please don't,' he said. Then he walked on, and climbed up on the chair; they put the rope around his neck and took away the chair. And, oh, God, how he kicked and thrashed around; he couldn't even die quickly! And I had to go on living . . . and remembering." Hilary was sobbing wildly by this time.

"You loved him?" Ian asked, when she was quieter.

Hilary turned around furiously, her eyes swollen.

"Loved him? I didn't love him! That's why what I did was so vile! There might have been some excuse if I'd loved him; not much, but some. I didn't, though. I don't even believe in God, but there must be something that sees to it that you get a punishment to fit your crime. Two months after Anatol's death, I found I was pregnant."

"Hilary, no!" Ian exclaimed. "What on earth did you do?"

"Well, I couldn't bear the child of a man I had practically hanged with my own hands. I was a nurse, if you remember. When we missed the submarine I thought the chances were that I was going to die anyway but, to be on the safe side, I aborted myself. Unfortunately, I didn't do a very good job. The surgeon at the hospital must have wondered just what had happened but, aside from telling me that I could never have any children, he never asked me questions. I've never had a wild urge to have children . . . except yours. Since that was out of the question . . ." Hilary shrugged.

"So that was why you'd never marry me!" Ian said reflectively.

"The chief reason. At the time, too, I felt—well—unclean; I didn't think I could ever marry anyone. And I knew children were important to you; I wanted you to have a normal life."

"You know, Hilary, trying to arrange other people's lives rarely works out. It was you I wanted. You left me and I married a beautiful bitch who presented me with two children, neither of whom has the slightest desire to consider me their biological father."

"What on earth makes you think that?"

"I know it," Ian said grimly. "I was in the ell of the library the other day, reading. Jeremy and Merise came in and sat on the window seat talking, not realizing I was there. Together they reviewed all Isabelle's 'intimates' in an effort to figure out which might have been their respective fathers. From the way they talked, it sounded as though this speculation was a frequent subject of conversation. Apparently it never even occurred to them that they might have been sired by the same man."

"What an extraordinary thing to overhear!"

"I thought so."

"How did you rank as a possible biological father?"

"I wasn't even in the running. It's going to be quite a disappointment to Jeremy when he begins to realize that he is getting to look more and more like me. I gathered he's hoping his father is the Duke of Walshingham because he's so horribly rich. Merise is torn between two possible fathers: Lagalishe, that French actor or singer or whatever he is, and Jack Sutton, owner of the famous Sutton stud. Merise likes horses," Ian added drily.

"What's your opinion?"

Ian shrugged.

"I've lost interest. I'm pretty certain Jeremy is my son if only because we both have three crowns, which make our hair grow in odd directions. But since the only reaction I ever get when I try to talk to him is cold, sullen politeness, I leave him alone. I don't really care much for either child."

"But why did you choose Isabelle to marry? The whole of London could have told you that she was more or less a nympho."

"Ambition. I wanted to prove something or other, possibly to you but more likely to myself. You have to remember that you turned down my offers of marriage over and over again and, of course, I didn't know why. When you'd gone to India I found out how rich you were and I decided the reason you wouldn't marry me was that you didn't think I was good enough. So I married the richest, best-connected, most beautiful woman in England just to show you! What a fool I was!"

"Have you never thought about divorce?"

"When you marry into the royal family, even peripherally," Ian said, "you owe it to them not to cause embarrassment. It's true that divorce is gradually being accepted by them but they still don't like it. So, unless *you* marry me, I don't believe I'll be the cause of the sort of scandal that would result from divorcing Isabella. Would you marry me if I were free?"

Hilary shook her head.

"No," she answered. "Why upset a perfectly good relationship? We have mutual interests, see each other whenever we want to, still have a good time in bed and, on my side at least, something that is much stronger than affection. How many of the people we've known over the years are still married to their original partners for as many years as we've been together?"

"Damn few," Ian admitted.

"Why change things, then?"

"Probably you're right." There was a lengthy silence. "You've made me feel horribly guilty, Hilary. I had no idea of what you went through in Greece. You must have forgiven me for getting you into such a situation a long time ago and I can only wonder at your magnanimity."

"What nonsense! There are certain things in life people have to be willing to suffer and to die for. I've never regretted what I did. But I probably shouldn't have kept it bottled up so long. Now that I've told you, I feel at peace, really at peace, for the first time. Confession is one of the advantages Catholics have over other people. I suppose the penitent comes out of the confessional feeling as though his soul has been scrubbed clean."

"And all ready to start over again?" Ian asked.

"Probably. The confessional isn't any more likely to turn out saints than the psychiatrist's couch is."

"At least it's cheaper."

"It must be frightfully boring for the priest, though. Imagine having to listen to accounts of all those dreary little sins for hours!"

"I don't know. I imagine most priests would have found your story quite interesting! According to the blurbs on the cover, readers of *Blood for Drachmas* are lapping it up."

CHAPTER 9

In the spring of 1965 Hilary was again in India. She and Ian were to meet in Persia and then fly to France to spend some time together in Brittany. But in Calcutta Hilary got a cable from Ian telling her that he had to go back to England immediately.

With time on her hands, Hilary decided to fly to Hong Kong and then on to California.

When she arrived at the Los Angeles airport a few days later, she stunned her aunt and her cousin with her chic. As a girl, she had paid little attention to her clothes; the best that could ever have been said about her garments was that they were of good quality. Now her black hair, which she used to wear in a heavy bun, was cut to fit her head like a gleaming skullcap, in points on either cheek. The expression in her green eyes was slightly sardonic and she still had the impish mouth of a small monkey; she had an interesting, alert face—what the French might call a *jolie-laide*. Her well-made black suit was piped in red lizard, and she had red lizard shoes and handbag.

"Hilary!" her aunt exclaimed. "I hardly knew you. You look wonderful!"

"Thank you," Hilary said as she kissed her. Then she turned to kiss her cousin. "You're living up to your name,

Felicia! You look very happy. Oh, it's wonderful to see you, darlings! How are the children?"

"Just fine. Carlino is twelve now, you know."

Hilary looked confused. "Who is Carlino?" she asked. "Did you have another child?"

"No, but when Carl adopted Timothy, we decided to change his name to 'Carl, Jr.,' and we call him 'Carlino' to avoid confusion with his stepfather."

"Felicia, he's going to be 'Timothy' to me. That's how I always think of him. I can't call a boy by a silly name like Carlino!"

"That's what I tell her," Mrs. McDougal said.

"Oh, Mother! It's a small enough matter and it pleases Carl," and Felicia's voice had an edge to it.

This interchange put something of a damper on the conversation. Hilary, changing the subject, chatted about Hong Kong and her trip till they reached Mrs. McDougal's house, where Felicia's husband was waiting for them.

"My new cousin!" Carl Dessein exclaimed, greeting them at the door and holding Hilary in a bear hug that almost suffocated her. "Welcome to California! Felicia, you never told me she was a beauty. You've been keeping things from me!" and he wagged an admonitory finger at his wife.

"Well, she didn't use to be," Felicia replied a bit tartly.

Hilary, looking at Carl Dessein, realized she had never taken such an instant, intense, and irrational dislike to anyone in her life.

"Where are the children?" she asked.

"You'll see them when you come here tomorrow. We

decided that this evening would be for adults," Felicia replied.

Hilary had arranged to rent a car and the next morning she drove herself over to her cousin's house, taking the presents she had brought for the three children, who were there to greet her.

"I'm not going to carry on about how you've grown, which always seemed the silliest remark I'd ever heard when I was a child. I once got into trouble by answering 'Well, you'd be pretty surprised if I hadn't.' If you go out to the car, you'll find three packages. Since I didn't know what sort of things you liked, I can only hope I did all right."

"Oh, you shouldn't have brought them anything; they're spoiled enough as it is," Carl said.

Hilary looked at him appraisingly.

"Well, there aren't many times in life one gets a chance of being spoiled. One should make the most of them, don't you think?"

"I don't know about that. You look like a pretty spoiled little lady to me."

"Do I?" Hilary replied and turned to greet her aunt, who had just come in.

The phone rang and Felicia went into the next room to answer it.

"It's an overseas call for you, Hilary," she said as she came back. "You can pick it up in Carl's den."

"I can't get over how wonderful Hilary looks," Mrs. McDougal said as her niece left the room. "She's getting to look more and more like her mother as she gets older."

"Well, I like a little more substance myself," Carl said, putting an arm around his wife and drawing her to him as they sat on the sofa.

"No bad news, I hope?" Carl asked when Hilary returned.

"No, not really," she replied, looking reflective.

The desultory conversation that followed was punctuated with half-suppressed giggles in the hall as the children examined their presents. Finally the three of them filed back into the drawing room, dressed in Indian clothes.

"Don't you all look splendid!" Hilary exclaimed.

"That material is beautiful!" Felicia said. "Come here, Jacqueline. Let me look at that sari more closely. It's all hand-embroidered, isn't it?" she asked her cousin.

"Yes, it is. And that's real silver. When the saris finally wear out, which sometimes takes a few generations, they are burned and the gold and silver used in the embroidery is salvaged. A woman I knew had a solid-silver coffee table made of what had been recovered from her family's saris. Timmy, come over here and I'll help you with your turban. They're kind of hard to fix. You start like this . . ."

Just then the maid came in to announce lunch.

"Mother, can we eat in these clothes? Please let us!" Timothy begged.

"Oh, I think you'd better change into your own things. You might spill something on that beautiful velvet," Felicia said.

"Those clothes must have had heaps of things spilled on them," Hilary said, "they're nearly a hundred years old.

That outfit Timothy has on was made for the young son of the Maharajah of Jaipur at the time of Queen Victoria's Jubilee."

"In that case, the children should take off those clothes *immediately*. They're probably covered with germs. We'll have them fumigated before we let the children play with them," Carl said.

"Yes, children. Carl is quite right. Get out of those things *at once*."

Walter looked rebellious, Jacqueline looked sulky and Timothy began to cry, but none of the children moved to obey.

"It's probably too late now," Jacqueline said. "We've probably caught whatever it is we're going to catch. So we might as well enjoy ourselves till we get sick."

"Carl, are you going to take them upstairs or shall I?"

"I'll take them, darling. Don't wait for me."

"Tell Nanny to shut them up in their rooms without any lunch," Felicia said. "I'll deal with them later."

"Well, I must say, Felicia, you put me in a damned uncomfortable position," Hilary said after Carl and the children had gone. "You don't think I'd have given the kids those clothes without having them cleaned, do you?"

"Did you have them fumigated?"

"Well, no. I wouldn't even know how to set about having them 'fumigated.' But I'm reasonably sure no one is going to come down with bubonic plague."

"You don't have any children so, naturally, you don't realize how easily they catch things."

"I may not have any children but, as a nurse, I do know a little about contagious diseases."

"Oh, let's talk about something else," Mrs. McDougal said crossly. "I think you've made a ridiculous fuss about nothing, Felicia. Let's have lunch without waiting for Carl. If his is cold, it'll serve him right for starting all this."

The three sat down to their meal but the atmosphere was still rather strained and, for women who hadn't seen each other for so long, they had surprisingly little to say. Carl got back in time for coffee, and when he sat down the temperature seemed to drop two or three more degrees.

"What are you doing tomorrow?" Mrs. McDougal asked Hilary, paying no attention to him.

"I've arranged with the storage people to go through the boxes tomorrow, and I expect I'll send most of the stuff to the auction rooms. You're sure it won't bother you to have a few things in your attic, Felicia? Auntie told me it would be all right."

"Yes, of course. Our attic's only got a few empty suitcases in it. What do you want to leave?"

"There's Mother's silver. When and if I finally settle down in London, I'll send for it. There's also a good deal of furniture, but that, unless you can use it, I plan to sell."

"We've got all the furniture we need," Felicia replied.

"There are also vast quantities of hand-embroidered linen, most of which Mother inherited. You can have any of it that you want."

"I don't think I want any, Hilary."

"I'll sell all that, then. The only other things I intend to keep are the big Bible from Father's family and Mother's portrait that was painted by Shadrac about five years before she was killed. It's sheer sentiment that makes me keep the Bible; what I should do is send it to my great-uncle's family in Yorkshire. But Mother and Father toted that great, heavy thing around the world and I sat on it after I graduated from a high chair but was still too small to get my head above the dining room table when I sat on an ordinary chair. I'll leave it to the Yorkshire Tarrants in my will."

"Is it an old one?" Carl asked.

"Yes, very. It's a Caxton Bible, as a matter of fact, printed in Bruges in the middle of the fifteenth century, and it's very valuable. It didn't come into the Tarrant family until seventeen-eighty, though. I don't remember whom it belonged to before that, if I ever knew.

"About Mother's portrait, Father ordered it to help Shadrac, who was an unknown painter then and was having trouble getting enough to eat. Father could hardly tell the difference between an oil and a watercolor, but he liked Shadrac, who was touchy about taking handouts. So he ordered the portrait. It turned out to be an outstanding specimen of his work, which is bringing in fabulous sums these days. A still-life of his sold for two hundred and eighty thousand dollars the other day."

"There are some pieces of Mother's jewelry in the safe deposit box at the bank," Hilary went on. "I'm going to turn those over to you to give the children when they are twenty-one."

"I must say this is very generous of you, Hilary," Carl said. "The children will be most grateful and I thank you in their name."

Hilary, feeling that she couldn't stand being in the

same room with Felicia's husband another minute, got to her feet.

"I guess I'd better get back to the hotel to rest. I've got quite a schedule. Can you and Felicia come to have lunch with me tomorrow, Aunt Louise?"

"I'd love it," Felicia said.

"Oh, but, sweetie, isn't tomorrow the day of the cancer committee meeting at the hospital?"

"Goodness! Thanks for reminding me, darling. It had completely slipped my mind."

"Can't you skip a committee meeting just once?" Hilary asked, a trace of irritation in her voice.

"The trouble is that I'm the chairman and this is an important meeting; we're going to fix the budget for the coming year."

"If you can't you can't. Auntie, I'll expect you at the hotel anytime after eleven. I'll order lunch upstairs. Felicia, perhaps you and I can get together the day after tomorrow."

"Yes, of course. I'll give you a call."

"By the way, Cousin Hilary," said Carl, "were you able to get the tussore for me in Hong Kong? Felicia said she wrote you about it."

"Yes, I have it at the hotel; I just forgot to bring it."

CHAPTER 10

"Tell me about Felicia's husband," Hilary said the next day when the waiter had gone and the two women were sitting down to lunch in her suite at the Beverly Wilshire.

"What do you think of him?"

"I just hope, for his sake, that I don't have to watch any more performances like the one he gave yesterday."

"I have to admit that Carl wasn't at his best; it's the first time I've seen him carry on like that. He's usually very friendly."

"It seems obvious to me that he married Felicia for what he thought he could get out of her."

"Hilary, that's just your prejudice," Mrs. McDougal said crossly. "Carl has money of his own."

"How much?"

"Naturally, I don't know just how much. Enough, I fancy. And, until he quit his job, he had his salary from the institute."

"Why did he quit? He's surely not old enough for retirement. In one of her first letters to me after she'd married Carl, Felicia told me how wonderful it was to have a husband who wasn't underfoot all the time. If he hasn't got a job, that accounts for the fact that he's anxious to get his hands on some capital."

"I don't know that he's trying to do any such thing!"

"*I* know, though," Hilary answered. "It all started this morning, before I left to go to the storage warehouse. I got a call from Felicia, who said she'd thought things over and it seemed such a pity to let all those lovely things go out of the family. She'd like to be able to give the children heirlooms when they set up housekeeping, so, instead of going to the auction room, she proposed that all the stuff go from the warehouse straight to her attic. Instead of not wanting *any* of the things, now she wants them all. You can't tell me that isn't Carl's doing."

"It's certainly strange," Mrs. McDougal admitted. "Are they going to pay you for what they're taking?"

"It seems unlikely. Naturally, I don't want to be paid and I did offer to let her have anything she wanted. But I was a bit stunned when she said she'd take it all. I don't know that I particularly want to hand Carl several thousand dollars. How did you come to let her marry him?"

"I had nothing to do with her marrying him. Felicia's a grown woman."

"Oh, come off it, Aunt Louise. Felicia's never done anything in her life on her own. You've been right there every step of the way."

"I certainly had nothing to do with her marrying that worthless Walter Simmons," Mrs. McDougal said sharply.

"I was going to ask you about him. What is he doing now? Does he ever see the children?"

"Certainly not! We never permit him to be mentioned in their hearing."

"I think that's wicked, Aunt Louise! There was nothing so terrible about Walter . . . he was just weak. I think most of the trouble was your fault."

"*That's ridiculous!* I wasn't the cause of his signing bad checks."

"In a way, you were. You gave him a taste for a life-style he had no means of sustaining. If you'd left him alone, he'd have been a happy veterinarian in some small farming community. Do you mean you have no idea where he is?"

"I do know where he is," Mrs. McDougal admitted. "I thought I ought to keep an eye on him in case he became an embarrassment . . . took to a life of crime or something like that."

"And did he?"

"Apparently not. He married a widow who owned a wholesale hardware business; she put him through veterinary school and he's now living in Minnesota," Mrs. McDougal answered unwillingly.

"You see?" Hilary said triumphantly.

"That wouldn't have been much of a life for Felicia."

"I don't know. What's so marvelous about her life now?"

"Never mind about Felicia and her problems. Tell me about yourself. Your travelogues are on TV a lot these days. You must be making a good deal of money. What do you do with it all?"

"The profits go to the children's hospital run by the nuns in Calcutta I once told you about. But the travelogues today don't net as much as the old ones did. I have to hire people for things that Mother and Father did themselves and, anyway, costs have spiraled. In the East, too, bribery is a way of life and I have to grease so many palms to get government permits to make the films. If I didn't bribe, I have a raft of foreign competitors who wouldn't hesitate for a second to do so."

"Aren't you ever going to get married?"

"I doubt it, Auntie. Not till I'm a good deal older—say about fifty-five. I should think twenty years of living together must be about as much as any two people can stand. And, with longevity being what it is, fifty-five would be just about right to start."

"Let me tell you, my dear, that it isn't easy to find a husband when you get to that age."

"With all my money? You've got to be kidding!"

"You don't want to *buy* a husband."

"Why not? If you're careful, you at least know what you're getting."

"You know, I rather hoped that you'd end by marrying that terribly good-looking Major Maitland."

Hilary, who was clearing the lunch dishes from the table and stacking them on the waiter's trolley, turned around and stared at her aunt.

"How on earth do you know anything about Ian Maitland?" she asked.

"Don't you remember my visit to you when you were so ill?"

"Of course I remember; you practically saved my life. But Ian had nothing to do with that."

"How do you suppose I knew you were ill? Or how I managed to get transportation to Europe in wartime? It was Major Maitland who sent for me and arranged it all."

"He never said a word to me!"

"No, I don't suppose he did. He told me not to say anything, either. But I figured it wasn't important anymore, after all these years. Do you still see him?"

"Yes. We're very good friends."

"Do you still work for that intelligence organization?"

"They went out of business after the war ended."

"Don't quibble. I may not be an intellectual giant but I'm no fool, either. I've watched the news, noted where your letters came from and tried to guess what you were doing. I should think the travelogues would make a very good cover."

"I still do occasional jobs," Hilary admitted reluctantly.

"I expect it's interesting work, dear."

"Rarely. It's not at all like in those novels you read. I know, because I read them, too. For instance, my last job consisted of reading in Farsi everything a mullah, who was stirring up trouble on the Afghan-Iran border, had published in the last ten years. Trying to make a précis of his convoluted prose was one of the most sleep-inducing jobs you can imagine."

"Why was what he had to say of any importance?"

"There seems a pretty good possibility that the man may become a powerful figure in that part of the world so Ian felt we should know a little about his political philosophy. Very few statesmen in Europe took the trouble to read *Mein Kampf*, which clearly set forth Hitler's ambitions and plans; Ian feels that this oversight shouldn't occur again in the section of the world that is his intelligence responsibility." Hilary began to laugh. "Bits of it were quite interesting, in a scatological way," she went on. "There were pages about the depth of penetration into the vagina permitted during periods of religious fasts. Too deep penetration, according to the old boy, would negate the spiritual value of the fast. Presumably you went to bed with a tape measure." Hilary stood up. "I've got to throw you out, Auntie. I have an appointment at three-thirty."

"How long are you going to be in California?" Mrs. McDougal asked as she rose to her feet.

"About another ten days. I'm having lunch with Felicia the day after tomorrow. She seems very busy these days and couldn't make it any sooner."

"For goodness' sake, Hilary, don't say anything against Carl to her."

"Of course I won't! What do you take me for?"

"A tactless, opinionated woman given to sweeping judgments; that is, unless you've changed, which seems unlikely."

"I don't suppose I have changed but I don't shoot off my mouth as much as I used to. Anyway, Felicia's marriage is her own business and I hope she's happy."

"I think she is, you know. Call me when you have a minute," Mrs. McDougal said, kissing her niece.

CHAPTER 11

Hilary, on her way to her appointment, remembered to stop off at the bank to have the jewelry she had promised Felicia's children transferred to them. She had just returned to the hotel and was preparing to take a shower when the telephone rang.

"This is Carl, Cousin Hilary," a male voice said. "I was quite near the hotel and thought I'd stop by to say hello. At the same time, I could pick up the tussore Felicia told me you were kind enough to buy for me in Hong Kong. And, if you've got them there, I could perhaps save you some trouble by picking up the Bible and the portrait of your mother. I have the station wagon with me."

"Where are you now?"

"Down in the lobby."

"I'm just taking a shower now, Carl. Can you wait about a quarter of an hour before you come up?"

Hilary swore mildly as she finished drying herself and slipped into a thin cream colored wool robe. She had just combed her hair when there was a knock at the door.

"Sorry to have kept you waiting," Hilary said as she opened it. "Come on in."

"I should apologize for dropping in on you, Cousin Hilary."

"Sit down. What would you like to drink? All I have is

gin and some tonic water but I can send down to the bar for anything you like."

"Gin and tonic sounds fine, but not too much gin. I'm not a great drinking man. Can I get it for you?"

"Don't bother. I shan't be a minute."

Hilary came back with two drinks and handed Carl one.

"Look, Carl, how about skipping the 'cousin' business? Just plain 'Hilary' will do fine."

"Never 'plain'!" Carl replied with a courtly bow. "But I shall be proud to call you Hilary."

"I'll fetch the tussore," she said, getting up. "As for the Bible and the portrait, they're coming in the truck with the rest of the things."

"Felicia felt that family heirlooms should stay in the family. I must compliment you on the robe you have on. The embroidery is magnificent."

"I'm fond of it myself. My father bought it for my mother the first time they went to India. It's Kashmiri work and very beautiful."

"Could I look at it more closely?" Carl asked, getting up. "Don't laugh, but embroidery is my hobby. Perhaps I could make a drawing of the pattern some time and try to copy it. I'd like to make a robe like that for Felicia."

"The trouble is that you wouldn't be able to get the wool. Even in Kashmir it's not made anymore. It's so fine that, before it's embroidered, a yard of it can be run through a wedding ring. You could try some other material, though," Hilary answered, undoing the belt of the robe and handing it to him. "The whole of the motif is here; it's repeated on the rest of the robe in various sizes."

Taking out a notebook, Carl sketched the motif in incredibly tiny detail.

"How beautifully you did that!" Hilary said as she replaced the belt.

"I'm glad you approve of something about me," Carl replied.

"What on earth do you mean?" Hilary asked, startled.

"I would have thought it was unlike you to be hypocritical," he answered. "I have the feeling you dislike me; I can't help wondering why."

Hilary was silent for a minute.

"I hardly know you," she finally said. "I have no very strong feeling of like or dislike."

"But you tend toward the dislike. Why?"

"Assuming you're right, and I'm not saying you are," Hilary answered coolly, "don't you think it might be because you're capable of asking a question, like that, which naturally embarrasses me?"

"No, I wouldn't say so," Carl answered reflectively. "I'd say plain speaking was your thing."

"You've gathered this from our very brief conversations?"

"Not entirely, of course. Felicia and her mother have talked about you a good deal. They both told me that you had always been very outspoken, which is why I asked my question."

"They haven't seen much of me since I was fairly young," Hilary said drily. "Years never change one's basic character, but one does learn to conceal some of one's minor faults. Did you come to see me merely to ask me why I didn't like you?"

"Not entirely. Felicia told me you proposed taking the children to lunch and then to Humperdinck's *Hansel and Gretel.*" Carl Dessein paused for a moment.

"Yes."

"I'd like to ask one thing and that is that you promise not to mention their father to them."

Hilary frowned. "I hadn't considered the matter of our subjects of conversation. But if one of them should want to talk about his father, I should certainly go along. What's the harm? There was nothing terribly wrong with Walter except that he was young and a little weak. The way you and Aunt Louise and Felicia carry on, one would think he had murdered somebody."

Carl Dessein reddened.

"I don't consider writing large checks on someone else's bank account a very praiseworthy action."

"Certainly not praiseworthy; it was a foolish, juvenile thing to do. You have to remember, though, that it was, by law, his bank account as well as Felicia's. But never mentioning Walter's name, letting the children think he's dead, seems absurd beyond belief. They'll find out someday and get all kinds of complexes. Was it Felicia's idea to have you be her messenger in this matter? Why doesn't she speak to me about it herself?"

"She's afraid of you."

"Now you're being absurd."

"Afraid you'd disapprove," Carl amended.

"She's quite right about that. She must realize, then that what she's doing is wrong. Why do it?"

"She feels, and I agree, that the children should think

of me as their father and not be reminded of the fact that, biologically, they had another."

"You came on the scene too late for that. Tim probably doesn't remember Walter but the two eldest certainly do. And Tim probably thinks he does from having heard the others talk about him."

"So you refuse to promise?"

"I'm willing to promise I won't raise the subject. I won't promise not to answer any questions they put to me. Not that I know much about Walter. But children, particularly boys, have to be able to be proud of their parents and there was a good deal about Walter that was admirable: his kindheartedness, his love of animals, his good nature, and also his excellent war record; they have a right to know about all that."

"You're entitled to your opinion, but Felicia and I feel otherwise," Carl said, getting up. "So we think it better if you don't see the children again."

Hilary, too, rose to her feet.

"Did Felicia ask you to tell me that?"

"I'm afraid she did."

"Or is it all your idea?"

"Ask her."

"I think I shall."

"She may well tell you more—that she doesn't think Jacqueline, who is at an impressionable age, should be influenced by someone whose philosophy of life is so much at variance with Felicia's own."

"My God! Do you always talk like this? It all sounds very unlike Felicia, who I doubt ever thought of having a 'philosophy of life.' I imagine most of this is your doing, though what it's all for I can't think. We'll bring this tiresome conversation to a close and, so far as I'm concerned, you can go to hell! Goodbye, Mr. Dessein!"

As Carl got in his car and started the motor, he looked well pleased with himself.

When Hilary called her cousin, the conversation was brief. Felicia embarrassedly confirmed what Carl had said.

"Oh, you can go to hell, too!" Hilary finally exclaimed angrily as she crashed the receiver down. She left for Europe the next day, barely taking the time for a brief farewell visit to her aunt on the way to the airport.

CHAPTER 12

In the years during which Hilary worked for the intelligence group of which Ian Maitland finally became the head, she accepted assignments only when she felt she had special skills which were not easily obtainable elsewhere.

"I want to be free to turn down jobs," she said. "I don't want to be on the payroll."

"But we have to have control of your activities when you're working," Ian's predecessor had said.

"I recognize that and if I agree to undertake something, I'll always obey orders. But I want to limit my work solely to information-gathering and don't want to get involved in active manipulations.

"Anyway," she went on, "my own experience has brought me to the conclusion that, while a nucleus of career employees is necessary for an intelligence agency, a large staff is self-defeating. As soon as you make intelligence work a career, you open a whole Pandora's box of troubles—ambition, jealousy, self-serving, greed—all disastrous for good intelligence work. The best way to operate an organization like ours is to gather together a group of dedicated persons who have the kind of minds to become absorbed in the work for its own sake rather than for the remuneration it offers."

"It's also, of course, the cheapest way," Ian added.

Hilary Tarrant and her team had taken on the rather daunting task of filming the most dramatic episodes of Thucydides' history of the Peloponnesian War. In these, Hilary tried to bring out the analogy between ancient Greece and modern Europe: both fighting unwanted but unavoidable wars, both struggling to make the ideal of democracy viable only to be defeated by dictatorships, both having to face embittered class struggles and revolution. As Greece's Golden Age dimmed and died, so, and for the same reasons, Hilary's films implied, would Western civilization.

The work had taken nearly a year and Hilary was tired. When the rest of the crew flew back to New York, Hilary rented a yacht and, after a leisurely cruise through the Aegean, sailed for Brittany, where she telegraphed Ian Maitland to join her.

"Do you realize I haven't kissed you for over a year?" Ian said as he took her in his arms. "I've missed you all day and every day."

"Nonsense!" Hilary replied briskly. "Half the times I called, your secretary said you were out of the country."

"Well, yes. I've had to do quite a bit of traveling."

"Interesting?"

"Hard work. I wish someone would do away with all publishers, preferably by boiling them in oil. Because of Wentworth Eyre's damn memoirs *My Years as a Spy*, we've had to change most of our agents in Turkey, Iraq and Lebanon. That bookkeeper never had anything to do with intelligence-gathering; all he did was handle the payroll. It's infuriating to see how the worst aspects of American life seem to float across the Atlantic; I had thought the CIA had the monopoly on self-seeking psychos on the make."

"Poor Ian!" Hilary laughed.

For several days they played golf, went fishing and sailing and ruined packs of cards playing bitterly contested games of Double Demon.

"What are your projects?" Ian asked casually one morning as he folded and put away a letter he had just received.

"When I feel completely rested, I'll go to London to do some research on Empedocles to see if we could make an interesting film on his life. We've never used Sicily for background; in fact, I've never been there. If there isn't, I suppose we'll have to undertake a project I've been dubious about, on Socrates."

"Did he ever do anything filmable? I thought his chief occupation was talking—all those dialogues."

"That's the reason I've been avoiding the project. But there has been a good deal of pressure on me from various scholastic groups who have promised their assistance."

"How much time do you have before you have to start work again?"

"A month or so. Why?"

"To tell the truth, I need you."

"I thought we'd agreed I'd been pretty much phased

out except in emergencies when it was impossible to find someone else," Hilary said with a frown, after a lengthy pause. "Is this an emergency?"

"Not exactly. But it's an opportunity and it's unlikely to recur; my intuition tells me we should make the most of it."

"What is it?"

"Do you remember the abstracts you did of the two books by that mullah in Iran, Hassan Kayalli?"

"How could I forget that sexually obsessed scatological dreamer preaching a war to impose Islam on the world? Surely you can't be worrying about such a mad man!"

"The old boy is nearly sixty now and in all these years, despite a stream of wives, he's succeeded in fathering only one child, a daughter, Shahla, whom he adores. The girl has developed polio and is very ill; Hassan Kayalli, much as he hates all things Western, including Western medicine, is so frantic that he approached the British consulate in Tabriz to ask if it would be possible to find a Persian-speaking woman doctor in England who could save the child."

"I see what you have in mind," she said. "Do you think it's really worthwhile? Is there any reason to think the man will ever have any political following in his own country?"

"You know how things change overnight in that part of the world. The Shah might be thrown out again, as he was during the Mossadegh period, or he might be assassinated, and it's always a good idea to have contacts with the opposition."

"There is no specific job that you want me to do?"

"No. Just try to get to know the man as well as possible. And, of course, do the best you can for the daughter. It would be one way of putting Kayalli in our debt."

"What happens if he looks me up in the medical register and doesn't find me?"

"He knows no English and I doubt that he's that sophisticated. Anyway, it will be no problem; we'll fix you up with a diploma and provide you with the matching papers in the name of someone who is in the register."

"About the care of the girl, though. I'm no doctor."

"You're a damn good nurse and I've always heard that the nurse is more important than the doctor in cases of polio. Dr. Arthur Ridgeway, one of the leading authorities on the disease, has gathered the information you'll need in order to treat the child. He's going to fly with you as far as Beirut to tell you everything he can about what symptoms or complications to look for and what you should do if they occur."

"I take it that time is of the essence."

"Yes, it is. You and Ridgeway should leave London first thing the day after tomorrow."

The morning Hilary was to fly to Beirut on her way to Tabriz, Ian was at her flat well before six and let himself in with his key.

"Are you up?" he called.

"Only just," she answered from the bathroom. "Be an angel and put some coffee on."

Hilary came in and set down her suitcase. "Aren't you a mite early?"

"I wanted a minute to talk to you. Do you still carry a gun?"

"No. They're too much of a nuisance, given the security checks at airports on account of the skyjackings. It's embarrassing if you're stopped and have to answer awkward questions."

"It's because of that that we've had to develop a new weapon for our people and on this trip I think you should carry one. Since it's made of plastic, it naturally doesn't show up on the scanner."

"A plastic gun?"

"It's a weapon, but it's not a gun. Do you remember the death of Nicholas Krapotkin in Munich a few years ago?"

"That Russian spy who decided to work for us? Yes, I remember. He dropped dead, didn't he?"

"He was an apparently healthy man of thirty-two who suddenly suffered a fatal heart attack on the landing outside his apartment."

"Was he murdered?"

"He was murdered, all right. In his lungs the doctors found traces of a gas that paralyzes the heart. If the Germans hadn't gotten him on the autopsy table as fast as they did, all trace of the gas would have disappeared. A young boy coming home from school saw a man coming out of the apartment building throw something in the bushes. He retrieved it, and when the police showed up a few minutes later in answer to a telephone call from a neighbor who had found the body, he showed it to them and was also able to give a pretty good description of the man who had tossed it away. The murderer escaped but we succeeded in copying the weapon. Here it is."

"It looks like a toy," Hilary said as Ian showed her the little pink plastic gun.

"It's far from a toy. When you pull the trigger, what comes out is more lethal than a bullet, which can, and frequently does, miss its mark. This never does. To load it, you slip this little glass tube in this hole. To use it, you undo these two safety catches, push down on this button, which positions the poison gas, put a large handkerchief on your own nose and mouth, pull the trigger and then get away as quickly as you can." And Ian demonstrated as he talked. "Most important: be *sure* not to forget to cover your nose and mouth."

"You really think I have to have this, Ian? After all, I'm supposed to be on a mission of mercy."

"I'd be very much happier if you did."

"Well, all right," Hilary sighed. "Now we'd better leave if I'm going to make that plane."

An hour later Hilary and Dr. Ridgeway were on their way to Beirut, where they separated.

"Don't hesitate to call me if there's anything you need to know. I'll be available day and night; here's my telephone number," the doctor said as he left Hilary.

"I understand Hassan Kayalli considers the telephone a plaything of the devil. But I'll probably be able to get through to you somehow if I need to."

Hilary spent an arduous six weeks in the house of Hassan Kayalli. When the crisis of the polio attack had passed, she began making the child perform the various exercises which would help avoid the crippling effects of the disease, then trained the child's mother and some of the other women in the harem to continue them after she had gone.

Leaving, however, proved unexpectedly difficult. Shahla had developed a deep affection for her and had screaming fits, which she learned were effective, every time Hilary left her; the first time Hilary, discreetly covered by a chadar, tried to explain to the mullah that his daughter was now on the road to recovery and had no further need for her services, he turned a deaf ear. Hilary was apprehensive when Hassan Kayalli began to send for her more and more frequently and had her listen to long monologues. Thus she was not altogether surprised when he told her that he intended to marry her. She explained that she was barren and no suitable wife for Hassan Kayalli. Moreover, she added, she already had a husband. The mullah waved these arguments aside. That she was barren was, perhaps, unfortunate but in this case it would not prevent his marrying her since he would be doing it to ensure her continued care of his daughter. As for her husband, he would arrange for an Islamic divorce. He was, he said, leaving that evening for Kum, where an important meeting of mullahs was to be held; the wedding would take place on his return. He then indicated that the conversation was over.

Hilary returned to the women's quarters to consider how best to extricate herself from her present idiotic situation; leaving while the mullah was in Kum seemed indicated. But it also turned out to be impossible. One of his henchmen was guarding each door of the compound and firmly refused to let Hilary leave. She began to be afraid that she would have to use the weapon Ian had pressed on her in order to escape.

It was Shahla's mother who came to the rescue. Unenthusiastic about sharing her husband with yet another woman, she was more than eager to get this foreigner out of the place. Moslem women are, on the whole, a gregarious lot, so it was perfectly normal for Shahla's mother to arrange a gathering of her sisters and some other female relatives who came to the compound to spend the day. When it was time for them to leave, Hilary, dressed as one of the sisters, was among them, leaving behind all her things except the plastic gun.

Ian, when Hilary reported on her experiences, found them exquisitely humorous.

"It's all very well for you to laugh," Hilary said, annoyed. "If it hadn't been for the providential conference of mullahs in Kum, I might well have found myself in that fanatic's bed."

"You'd have been able to verify the statistics in his writings on how many centimeters the vagina may be penetrated for a man's religious fast to remain valid," Ian said. "And think of the money you'd have been able to make from magazine articles!"

"It wasn't so funny at the time," Hilary said soberly. "I began to be afraid the only way I would be able to get away was by using the gas gun. And I remembered Anatol von Rabenstein!"

"Darling, I'm sorry. It was thoughtless of me to laugh. At any rate, you seem to have got to know Hassan Kayalli quite well. How did he strike you?"

"I think you're right about the possibility that he may be dangerous. When he goes into one of his endless monologues, you realize there's no real intelligence there—just a mass of emotions. If he ever has anything to say about running his country—(and I imagine he may well prove an effective rabble-rouser)—God, or, rather, Allah, help Iran."

CHAPTER 13

Women's styles suddenly changed and Nanny Evans was sitting in the nursery shortening Felicia's skirts when she came into the room. Myfanwy Evans was a leather-faced Welshwoman, rawboned, flat-chested and of indeterminate age. She wore her white hair in an Edwardian style of considerable complexity and her various charges, over the years, loved to watch her as she combed her long hair and did it up. Her gray eyes, surmounted by heavy black brows, gave her face its character; they were both shrewd and kind. She had been with the family since Felicia was a baby. She had been about to go back to Wales to keep house for her mother's brother when Felicia, just married to Walter, found she was pregnant, and begged Nanny Evans to stay in the United States.

Felicia had been one of the Welshwoman's favorite charges and she loved the thought of taking care of her children, but she hesitated.

"I don't think I can do that, Felicia," she said. "I've got to think of my old age. Uncle Charley is going to make his house over to me and use his little capital to buy me an annuity; that, with my savings, will keep me quite comfortably."

"Oh, Nanny, you don't have to worry about the future. I'll take care of you."

"But what about when you no longer need me?"

"I'm *planning* to have a proper family, Nanny. I'm healthy, tough, and there's no reason I shouldn't have a dozen children—which ought to be enough to keep you busy for years. And this will always be your home, even after the children go off to school. You'll stay on and keep house for me; I'm sure I'll never be any good at it. We'll have tea together by the fire every afternoon and you'll teach me to make crumpets."

"California's kind of hot for fires and crumpets," Nanny Evans smiled.

"Please, Nanny. Isn't it pleasanter to be in California by the sea in the sunshine than in some grim little Welsh mining village? And now with this horrible war on I'd be surprised if it would be possible for you to get back to England. It would be dangerous."

"Oh, I think I can get passage back, though it may take a while. I was talking to a man at the English Club the other day and he says he thinks he can arrange something. And, as for the danger, I'm not going to let that worry me."

"Nanny, you can't leave me," Felicia wailed.

And, in the end, Myfanwy Evans stayed.

Now she looked up smilingly at Felicia.

"You've come just at the right time, dearie. I've basted these hems. Now I wish you'd try the skirts on," she said, shaking out the garment she had been working on and adding it to the others on a chair.

There was no answering smile on Felicia's face.

"Never mind about that now, Nanny," Felicia said. "I have something else I want to talk to you about. The other day, Mr. Dessein overheard you telling the children some wild story about how their father, when he was a boy, climbed up a burning water tower and put out a fire."

Myfanwy Evans looked at Felicia in surprise.

"Mr. Simmons' mother and father told me about the incident when they were visiting in Cambridge one Christmas when Mr. Walter was in law school. It happened in Virginia when Mr. Simmons was about fourteen. They had a summer place in a village on the Rappahannock. One of the houses there caught on fire, a wind came up and the fire began to spread. The fire brigade had been called, but before it could arrive the water tower caught fire. Since there was nothing the firemen could do without water, Mr. Walter covered himself with blankets and, with nothing but those and an old broom, succeeded in putting out the flames. You must have noticed the scars on his hands."

"That story is greatly exaggerated," Felicia said. "Anyway, I've told you repeatedly that I don't want you talking to the children about their father. You promised me you wouldn't."

"I promised you nothing of the sort, Felicia. When you first brought up the matter, not long after Mr. Simmons had gone, I told you I thought the idea of never mentioning their father to the children was foolish, but I agreed not to talk about him *unless they asked questions*. I've stuck to that."

"Nanny, they couldn't possibly have asked you about that silly burning water tower story. How could they have ever heard it?"

"Jacqueline was in the room when Mrs. Simmons was

telling it to me. She was old enough to understand. It was she who told the others."

"It seems to me, just the same, Nanny, that you've deliberately disobeyed me. Mr. Dessein says this particular case isn't the only one, but he didn't want to say anything to cause trouble."

Myfanwy Evans sniffed. "Perhaps it wasn't the only time. But I thought you'd realized by now that it's cruel to keep children from knowing about a parent regardless of what he's done."

"Well, I've had enough, Nanny. Mr. Dessein and I have talked the whole thing over and we agree that the children no longer need someone to take care of them. I think you spoil them, too; I know you're always picking up after them; they should learn to take care of their own things."

"I always did it for you, too, Felicia, and you don't seem to think you're any the worse for it."

"That is another matter. Anyway, I think it would be better if you were to leave us."

"Leave you?" The Welshwoman turned pale. "Why, where would I go?"

"I suppose you could find another job."

"At seventy-two?"

"Well, can't you go back to Wales? I'll pay your trip."

Myfanwy Evans' eyes narrowed.

"I was about to do that when you talked me into staying, Felicia. My uncle, of course, has died since then and he left his little property to the woman who took care of him. I have no one left in Wales. And now you're throwing me out after I gave up the promise of a home because you asked me to. I suppose this is Mr. Dessein's doing!"

"I think it's obviously time you left us," Felicia said coldly. "Mr. Dessein is goodness itself, and I don't want the children to hear anything against him. It's he who is their real father. And it was he who insisted that I give you a year's salary rather than the six months' which seemed to me more than adequate in view of the fact that you deliberately disobey all of my instructions."

Nanny Evans put her thimble down, stuck her needle into the pincushion and rose to her feet.

"Very well," she said briskly, "get your check ready. I'll have my things packed within an hour. I hope you'll carry your benevolence far enough to keep my trunk for me till I have an address where you can send it. Say goodbye to the children for me. I'll be gone before they get back from school."

"But, Nanny, I didn't mean you to leave right away!" Felicia exclaimed.

"Didn't you?"

"Of course not! You'll want to make arrangements. You can't just go like this!"

"'Watch my dust,' as the children say," Myfanwy Evans answered grimly.

When the children came home to find their beloved nurse gone, they felt bereft. Jacqueline turned sullen, locking herself up in her room for long periods of time till her mother removed the key; young Walter began to revolt against all authority, playing hookey from school and joining a band of neighborhood boys whose pranks sometimes brought them into conflict with the law. Only Timmy, after crying himself to sleep for a week, regained his sunny disposition and tried to win his mother's love to replace that of the departed nurse.

When Hilary was invited by the Turkish Government to visit the hospital she had helped set up in the early years of the war near Lake Van with a view to its modernization, she was pleased and extended her stay in the interior of Turkey to several weeks, traveling in parts of the country she had not ever seen. When she returned to England after this trip, she found in her mail a letter, dated more than a month earlier, from Mrs. McDougal. As usual, her aunt had indulged in her pet economy of saving on postage by cramming as many words as possible on a page of thin airmail stationery.

"I wish Aunt Louise would stop practicing writing the Lord's Prayer on the head of a pin when she writes to me," she said to Ian as she unfolded the letter and put on her glasses. "For God's sake!" she then exclaimed at the first words her eyes lit on.

"Has something happened?" Ian asked, lowering his newspaper.

"'So it's a miracle they weren't all burned to death,'" Hilary read aloud. "'If it hadn't been for the fact that old Mrs. Thatcher called the fire department as soon as she smelled smoke, it would have been too late. As you know, the Thatchers are Felicia's only near neighbors. The whole family left in their trailer for a weekend in the mountains, except for Mr. Thatcher's mother, who reneged at the last moment because her rheumatism was bothering her. If it hadn't been for that, Felicia and the children would probably have died.'"

"But how did it all happen?" Ian asked.

"I'd better start the letter at the beginning." There was a lengthy silence as Hilary deciphered her aunt's handwriting. "Well," she finally said, putting the letter down, "I seem to have been the biggest loser, financially speaking. Shadrac's portrait of Mother and the Tarrant family Bible presumably went up in smoke; nobody bothered to try to save the stuff that was in the attic. On the other hand, three months earlier Felicia had more than doubled the insurance on the house when Carl pointed out to her how underinsured she was in view of the huge increase in property values after the war. Now, until they can find somewhere else to live, the whole family has moved in with Aunt Louise." Hilary began to laugh. "Poor Auntie!" she added. "She says she's finding having children around the house twenty-four hours a day exhausting and she's encouraging Felicia to rent something until they decide about rebuilding."

"What caused the fire?"

"According to the newspaper clipping Aunt Louise enclosed, it was a short circuit by the fuel tank."

"That sounds rather odd to me," Ian said. "Where was the husband when all this happened?"

"Aunt Louise isn't too clear about this but, again from the clipping, which is from a Los Angeles paper, Carl was at his club. Even though he didn't get home until after the firemen had arrived, Aunt Louise says that if it hadn't been for his courage in forcing his way through the flames to reach Felicia and carry her out, she would have died. The firemen had found the children, who had wakened and were screaming, and carried them out through the windows. But Felicia was sleeping more soundly, and Carl saved her life. He was pretty badly burned, too, and was in the hospital for nearly two weeks."

"Where were the servants?"

"The couple they employ live in an apartment over the garage, separate from the house. And Nanny Evans apparently has left. I must say that surprised me, though I suppose the children are really too old for a nurse. But I thought I remembered that the arrangement was that Nanny would stay on with Felicia as a housekeeper."

"I've been thinking about the fire at your cousin's," Ian remarked over dinner. "I know a good deal about electrical engineering and I don't quite see how a short circuit by a fuel tank could have caused the thing to blow up unless the installation was done by an amateur. Any normal electrician would have used safeguards, precautions."

"I have to admit that a vague suspicion of arson has crossed my mind, too, but that could be because I took something of a dislike to Carl Dessein when I met him. Still, he's bound to know that, according to the terms of the trust, spouses of beneficiaries cannot inherit any trust income. So Felicia's demise wouldn't be to Carl's advantage—and I think his own advantage is the only thing Felicia's husband really cares about."

Hilary was very happy when she learned, in a subsequent letter from her aunt, that the Shadrac portrait and her family Bible had, in fact, been saved. There was, however, no trace of the silver.

Abe Stein had also read an account of the fire in the paper.

"I wonder if I was right in letting you persuade me not to warn Carl's second wife against him. I now feel I should have told her about Mother," he said, pointing out an article in the paper to his wife. "He doesn't seem to have changed his modus operandi."

"According to this article," Sonia said, "Carl Dessein saved his wife's life at the risk of his own."

"But the firemen had already arrived," Abe said.

CHAPTER 14

Before Felicia's children had fully recovered from the departure of Myfanwy Evans, the other mainstay of their life, Mrs. McDougal, died very suddenly. The whole family had been to her house for Christmas dinner. After her guests left, she had complained of stomach discomfort to Carrie, her cook, and commented on this folly of overindulgence in rich foods to celebrate the birth of a child in a manger approximately two thousand years earlier. She was found the next morning, lying on the bathroom floor. A broken glass, which had contained bicarbonate of soda, was beside her.

Hilary Tarrant knew nothing about the death of her aunt until she got a letter from Carrie some months later:

> I don't know when this will reach you, but I wanted to make sure you knew about your aunt's death. I was surprised that you didn't come to the funeral or even send any flowers, so I asked Felicia whether she had let you know; she went all hoity-toity on me and said that of course she had cabled and that you had answered that you couldn't get away. Now I've known you since you were a wee

child and sometimes you were a prickly little cactus but this just didn't seem like you, especially since there wasn't even a wreath from you and I made it my business to look. When I asked Felicia for your address (she and her husband had everything of Mrs. McDougal's sealed up as soon as the funeral was over so I couldn't look it up in your aunt's address book) she got real mad and told me to mind my own business. She's been mighty queer lately. Anyway, I called up the lawyer that handles the trust and he gave me the address of a bank which, he said, would forward my letter on to you. I surely hope you get it.

As soon as Mrs. McDougal's will was probated, Felicia and her husband took what they wanted from the house and the Trust had the rest of the things auctioned off (there weren't many left); then the house was put on the market and sold three weeks later. I've got a little cottage near the old place and I often drive by it. I bought Mrs. McDougal's little Volkswagen at the auction; she had promised to give it to me as soon as the new one she had ordered arrived. But, of course, she didn't put anything down in writing, and when I told Felicia she acted like she didn't believe me. So I bid for it at the auction. It still seems queer to me not to be living in the old house; I've spent most of my life there and know every nook and cranny in it.

I've always been careful with money and had saved enough for my old age, so after Mrs. McDougal died I intended to stop working and put my feet up but, mercy, a body gets bored without anything to do. So I started cooking for dinner parties now and then and people told each other about me; now I'm working harder than I ever did. But I'm my own boss, and when I feel like it I just say "no."

I wish I felt happier about Felicia's children. That husband of hers may mean well but those kids don't seem very happy to me and Timothy (they've finally given up that "Carlino" business) is getting to be a real handful. I don't know if it's true or not, but I heard he'd been picked up by the police, along with some other boys, for stealing a car. Now that Nanny's not with them anymore, those kids seem to run wild. Of course, they were pretty old to have a nurse, but Nanny was really more than that and I thought the way Felicia got rid of her was mean. She told Mrs. McDougal that Nanny up and left without so much as a day's notice and I just can't believe that. She must have been pushed to it somehow. It happened while Mrs. McDougal and I were in Bar Harbor for a couple of months. When we got back Mrs. McDougal tried to find Nanny, but she'd disappeared. I think Felicia only has daily help now. Hannah and Jake left and are working for the Ballisters; I see them occasionally. I don't guess you ever really knew them. Hannah's as closemouthed as a carp and will never say a word about why they quit. I think the kids must miss Jake—they were always following him around in the garden. Mr. Dessein does the work there himself now, and you've got to hand it to him. He does a real good job.

Well, Hilary, I sure hope this reaches you. Once I get started gossiping I can't seem to stop.

Yours truly,
Carrie J. Middleton

Hilary was in Calcutta when she received the letter. She was replacing the nun who ran the children's hospital, who had returned to France for several months to try to recover her health, much tried by the climate and by overwork. Tears came to her eyes when she learned of her aunt's death.

"This," she thought, "ends all connection with my youth. There's no one left now who loved Mother." When she reread the letter, however, she frowned. That she should not have received the cable Felicia had told Carrie she had sent was not surprising; what disturbed her was that she was supposed to have answered this communication, and she wondered why Felicia should have bothered to tell such a useless lie. As she folded the letter and put it aside, she was concerned by Carrie's remarks about Felicia's children and was particularly distressed by the fact that they no longer had Nanny Evans to rely on.

There was nothing she could do at that time, she decided. Anyway, Felicia's children were in no way her concern and Felicia would be the first person to tell her so. The two cousins had grown very far apart. Still, if her schedule allowed, she thought she might travel back to England via California. As it turned out, when she had finished her stint at the hospital, she got word that the producer who had taken over a lot of her work on the travelogues had been in an automobile accident and would be unable to work for months. So she flew straight back to Europe after writing Carrie a nice, newsy letter but not revealing Felicia's duplicity.

CHAPTER 15

Four more years passed. Ian's wife departed this world in a blaze of publicity when the small plane, in which she was returning from a Tunisian holiday with a lover twenty years her junior, blew up over the Channel. It took all Ian's efforts and the prestige of her family to suppress the fact that, in addition to fragments of two bodies, plastic bags full of a fine white powder were fished out of the water.

Though there was now no legal obstacle to their marriage, Hilary decided she preferred her independence. Her black hair had turned white with what she considered commendable celerity.

"I do dislike the pepper-and-salt stage," she remarked as she sat at her dressing table brushing her hair.

"I'm so happy you let it grow again," Ian said as he watched her. "I felt bereft when you had it cut."

She peered in the mirror. "The trouble with me is that I've lived in hot climates so much my face looks as if it were made of shoe leather," she went on. "And you're still so disgustingly handsome."

"I am, rather," Ian agreed complacently. "You have to admit that good looks are a great help to a man. Think how many copies of my memoirs will be sold simply because of my photograph on the cover! With a pipe, of course. A pipe is de rigueur and I've been practicing smoking one. I can't decide whether the kind that droops down or the straight one is more photogenic."

"Have you written your memoirs?"

"No, but I'm retiring next year and all secret service people write their memoirs when they retire. Some, particularly Americans, don't even wait that long. It would leave me open to the gravest suspicions if I were to keep silent. The world would think I had something to hide—that I had gone over to the Russians or was a homosexual or both. Of course, those people write their memoirs, too. In fact, those are the ones that make the most money. Perhaps I can think up a new vice to boost my sales."

"You're joking! You've always felt so bitter about the memoirs of intelligence agents."

"That was when they revealed secrets. Today there are no more secrets. The mechanical age has seen to that. What with satellites, computers, bugging devices and so forth, one's every thought is a matter of public record almost before one has had a chance to formulate it."

Hilary laughed.

"For a moment you almost had me fooled. I thought you really were going to write your memoirs."

"I probably won't but that's partly laziness. Memoir writing has become the major perk of public office. If prime ministers, presidents, cabinet officers, policemen and maybe trash collectors tell all after retirement in exchange for good-sized fortunes, why shouldn't I?"

"Trash collectors?"

"As far as I know, it's a virgin field. But, after your years of working with us, you must know that examining garbage is very revealing. I understand the cause of the last garbage collectors' strike in London was their inability to decide on an equitable distribution of the rights to the garbage of various singers, dancers, radio personalities and other celebrities. There's probably quite a bit that's salvageable and, for the lucky ones, plenty of promising material for blackmail."

Hilary laughed, getting to her feet. "I was out when the mail came. I'd better go see if I got any."

At dinner that evening in an Indian restaurant they frequently patronized, Hilary seemed distrait.

"Is something wrong?" Ian finally asked. "I've asked you twice for a chappati and you don't seem to hear."

"Oh, I'm sorry," she said, handing him the plate. "There's nothing exactly wrong; I't's just that I received a rather strange letter today. You know I've told you about my cousin Felicia."

"Yes, the one in California whose house burned down."

"Well, she doesn't write anymore. In fact, she never bothered to let me know her mother had died; the first I heard about it was in a letter from Carrie, who had been Aunt Louise's cook for years. Later, of course, I got word from the trust lawyers. The letter I received today was from a man named Abraham Stein whom I've never heard of. He wrote me about Felicia's son, Timothy. This Mr. Stein runs a chain of haberdashery stores in California and the other day he caught a boy shoplifting in one of them. Since this has been happening so much, he's become quite hard-hearted, he says, about calling the police. But he always talks to the culprit first to find out why he shoplifts. The boy seemed well educated and from a good family. In the course of the conversation, Mr. Stein discovered that his own former stepfather had married the boy's mother."

"That was an odd coincidence."

"Yes, it was. I met this man, Carl Dessein, who married Felicia, the last time I was in California and I perfectly understand anyone who dislikes him. I do myself. It's because of him that Felicia and I no longer correspond."

Anyway, Mr. Stein didn't turn the boy over to the police; he took him back to his own home instead. What Timothy told him in the course of the evening appalled him.

"Felicia's first husband was the boy's father. Felicia divorced him. It's what Mr. Stein tells me about all three children that's somewhat worrying. According to Timothy, Felicia and her second husband have thrown them out of the house."

"I've always heard that California is an odd sort of place but surely even there parents can't casually put their children out into the street."

"They're not literally in the street. Timothy was sent to a horrible boarding school."

"Darling, you've never had any children. To a boy, any boarding school is horrible. I went to what was really a very good school and thought I was persecuted."

"According to all the memoirs written by well-known Englishmen that I've read in the last few years, you undoubtedly were. There's a bit more to it than that, though. When Felicia dumped him at the school she sent instructions to the effect that her son was never to communicate with her in any way, and that the school should look after him during vacation periods."

"How long ago was this?"

"I gathered it was two or three years ago. And Felicia doesn't give Timothy any pocket money, so the only way he can get new clothes is to steal them."

"It sounds to me as though Timothy may be a second Ananias. Don't you think perhaps this Mr. Stein is just a gullible busybody?"

"It occurred to me. But wait till you hear the end. The boy has disappeared."

"Disappeared from where? The school?"

"Yes. Mr. Stein drove him back but promised to keep in touch. When he called two weeks later, he was told Timothy was no longer there."

"He had run away?"

"No. His mother had arranged for him to be taken to another school but the headmaster wasn't told where."

"Very curious. Do you think it's Stein who is the Ananias?"

"I can't see what he'd get out of making the whole thing up."

"How did he find your address?"

"Timothy gave him the address of the family's lawyers."

"Did he ask them what had happened to the boy?"

"Yes, he says he did. But I know that's a waste of time. You give that firm instructions and they follow them to the letter. I've told them to let anyone who asks for it have my address and they do. Felicia has given strict contrary instructions; nothing, but *nothing*, having to do with her or her family is to be revealed and no letter is to be forwarded. They communicate with her and ask if she wants to receive a particular letter. If she doesn't, it's returned to the sender. I found this out myself when, one Christmas, I decided to let bygones be bygones and wrote her a long letter. Since I wasn't sure she was at her old address, I sent it to the lawyers, asking that it be forwarded. The letter was returned to me with a very nice note from the head of the firm telling me that Felicia had instructed them not to send it on to her. So you see."

"Do you think she's got all her marbles?"

Hilary shrugged. "Anyway, Mr. Stein went to the trouble and expense of hiring a detective to try to find Timothy—so far, without success. So I feel I'd better go find out what this is all about. It'll mean putting off our vacation in Brittany till I get back. I hope you don't object."

"I object, but I know all about your overdeveloped sense of duty."

"It's not entirely a sense of duty. It's curiosity, too. I loved Felicia, you know, and I've missed not having any family since Aunt Louise died. So I think I'll fly over, probably by the end of the week."

Hilary got a call from Ian early the next morning.

"I assume you still have the plastic weapon I gave you when you went off to take care of Kayalli's daughter?"

"Heavens! I'd forgotten all about it! Yes, I do."

"In that case I wonder if you could do an errand for me on your way to California."

"What's the errand?" Hilary asked suspiciously. "I'm not going to assassinate anybody."

"Nothing like that. All I want you to do is go to California via Paris and give that gun to a Gerda Miller, who will be at the airport to meet you. Do you remember how to use it?"

"I guess so."

"You'll have to show her. Take her through the drill several times. It won't matter if someone sees you, that thing looks so much like a toy. If you leave London on the nine A.M. plane, you'll only have an hour's wait for your New York flight; that will be plenty of time. Is that all right with you?"

"I suppose so," Hilary answered. "How shall I recognize Gerda?"

"There will be a password."

"All right. I'll let you know as soon as my reservations are confirmed. Then you can get in touch with Gerda."

Hilary performed her part in this arrangement. Unfortunately, the electricians in France went on one of their periodic strikes that day and the whole of Paris became a gigantic traffic jam, since neither the Métro nor the suburban trains nor the traffic lights were functioning. Gerda Miller, stuck in her taxi, didn't reach the airport until two hours after Hilary's plane for California had taken off. So Hilary was unable to get rid of her lethal toy.

Hilary telephoned Abe Stein from New York and arranged to meet him at the Beverly Wilshire.

"I'm glad to meet you!" he exclaimed when Hilary opened the door to him. "I'd have insisted that you come to our place for dinner but Sonia is out of town and won't be back till Wednesday. She's playing in Minneapolis tonight."

"Playing?"

"Sonia plays the harpsichord and is giving three concerts in the Midwest."

"Then your wife must be Sonia Stein."

"Do you know her?"

"Not personally, but I've heard her play several times. The last time was at the Salzburg Festival two years ago."

"That's right. I was there with all six of our brats."

"Can I order you a drink?" Hilary asked.

"I'm not much of a drinker," he said. "I expect you want to hear about Timothy; there's a lot to tell."

"In your letter you said you'd hired a detective to find him. Did he succeed?"

"No, he didn't. But Timothy managed to smuggle a letter to me. He's at Kingswell School up in the northern part of the state. They wouldn't let me speak to him and my letter was returned."

"Had you ever heard of the school? What kind of place is it?"

"It's very well known here in California. You might describe it as a high-priced private reformatory."

"What about the other two children?"

"Timothy hadn't seen or heard from either of them for three years."

"I suppose what I should do is go see Felicia."

"Do you have her address?"

"Isn't she in the phone book?"

"They've moved and Timothy doesn't know where she's living. She may even have left the state."

"What about the old address? Won't the people who live there now give the new one?"

"The present owners say they don't know it. When Timothy wrote there the first year he was at boarding school the letter was returned by the post office marked 'addressee moved and left no forwarding instructions'!"

"What about Bel Air Institute, where Carl used to work?"

"I sent my detective there thinking that, if he had retired, they might have the address to which the pension checks were sent. The answer was that he had been with them less than two years when he was fired. There was, naturally, no question of a pension."

"This all sounds insane!" Hilary said, after a pause. "Why would they want to hide like this? There's got to be some way of finding them. How good is your detective?"

"His specialty is finding lost kids, not lost parents. In fact, it's usually the parents who are his employers. I couldn't tell him to go all out in his investigations because, of course, it was basically no concern of mine. But I've longed for years for the chance to get even with Carl Dessein. That bastard murdered my mother."

"He murdered your mother! When was this?"

"While I was a prisoner of war in Korea." And Abie Stein gave Hilary an account of what had happened.

"Of course, I dislike Carl Dessein so much I'm ready to believe the worst. But I suppose your mother's death could have been an accident. I don't see any real reason for him to have killed her."

"There were two hundred fifty thousand reasons, all green. And he probably didn't realize that her share of M & S was for her lifetime only and that when she died it would automatically come to me. Even I didn't know that. Mother was always very closemouthed about money matters."

"Still, I don't think you have enough to go on to be sure Carl murdered your mother."

"I learned more after I had been back home for a while. Among Mother's papers I found a bill from a lawyer she had consulted about a divorce."

"I see. That does make a difference. It would be very worrying, since we have no idea where Felicia is, if it weren't for the fact that her income which, since Aunt Louise died, must be in six figures, would stop with her death. Of course, anything she's saved—and Felicia was always careful about money—she can leave to whomever she likes."

"What happens to this income?"

"The principal goes back to the trust and it's divided among the rest of the heirs, including Felicia's children and me. So I would know if Felicia had died because my income would have changed. Also, the trustees would have notified me."

Abe Stein glanced at his watch and got to his feet.

"I have to get going," he said. "When Sonia is away, I like to be sure that all the children are safely tucked in. Keeping an eye on six, three of them teen-agers, is like trying to put your finger on mercury. Here are my telephone numbers, home and office," he added, handing Hilary a card. "Call me if there's anything I can do."

"You've already done so much," Hilary answered as she escorted her guest to the door. "I'll think things over; maybe the night will bring counsel. One trouble is that

I'm not in a strong position to do anything drastic, like going to the police. I'm only Felicia's cousin and if she chooses not to tell me where she's living, that's her right. I'll want to have a word with your detective and of course I'll work on the trustees. If we continue to butt our heads against a stone wall, I can probably get in touch with the children's father."

"Somehow I had the impression the father was dead."

"That's what the children were told. Perhaps he is now. But Aunt Louise told me he had remarried and was a veterinarian somewhere in Minnesota. He should be easy enough to find. Anyway, I'll be in touch. And thanks so much for everything you've done."

"It's been little enough; I'm very relieved that you've come."

Hilary's idea about how to flush out her cousin came to her while she was lying in the bath. As a result of it, she telephoned the law firm of Younghusband, Garnett & Morel and arranged for an appointment with Julian Morel, whom she had worked with when he was the OSS man attached to her intelligence unit right after the war.

"Hilary! I can't believe it!" Julian exclaimed, wrapping his arms around her in a hug that lifted her off the floor. "It's good to see you. You look wonderful!"

"I shan't be looking wonderful long if you don't put me down, Julian. You look fine yourself. I think you've grown; you're more ursine than ever."

"Any growing I've done has been sideways. How's that human hairpin, Ian Maitland? I read about the death of his wife and sort of half expected I'd read about the nuptials of the producer of Tarrant's Travelogues, but so far there hasn't been a line."

"I don't believe I'll ever get married, Julian. I've been a maiden lady too many years to give up my independence now."

"Still working for Ian?"

"Why, I quit to start up the travelogues while you were still with the OSS. You must remember that!"

"Oh, I remember all right. Thing is, I thought at the time those travelogues made much too good a cover for Ian's people not to make use of it. Don't bother to deny it, because I won't believe you."

"In that case, I won't," Hilary shrugged.

The lawyer picked up his phone and dialed.

"I don't want any interruptions, either telephone calls or anything else, until I let you know." He turned to Hilary. "Now tell me what I can do for you," he said quietly.

At seven P.M. they went out for half an hour to a snack bar and it was after midnight when Julian finally dropped Hilary off at her hotel.

CHAPTER 16

"Carl!" Felicia called out of the living room window to her husband, trimming a hedge in the garden. It had been some time since she had been able to control the pitch of her voice when she called out; in ordinary conversation she spoke in what might be called a loud whisper. Occasionally, when she had to speak loudly, her voice sounded more or less normal in her own ears; sometimes, though, it came out as a croak, at others all she could manage was a high-pitched whine, or, occasionally, a sudden deep, resounding bellow. Today seemed one of the good days. So she ventured a whole sentence. "Hilary has written to Livingston & Hill again," she went on.

Carl Dessein looked around from his work.

"You'd better close that window or you'll catch cold," he said. "I'll be right in."

Carl Dessein's gardening clothes, while peculiar, were certainly resplendent. He was dressed in pajamas made entirely of cloth of gold; on the back of the jacket was embroidered a magnificent rising sun, and smaller versions appeared on each sleeve.

Felicia's hands trembled a little as she obediently closed the window and made her way across the room in the walker Carl had built to make it possible for her to get around the ranch house he had designed.

The house was, in point of fact, a singularly unattractive one; its inspiration seemed to be pagodas out of Grauman's Chinese. Built of pearl-gray wood, it was decorated with particularly hideous factory-made gargoyles which were set about the tentlike roof. But the garden was a thing of great beauty.

"What did you say about your cousin, Hilary?" Carl asked as he came in from the kitchen, wiping his hands on a paper towel, which he then threw into the fireplace.

"She's written to Livingston & Hill again," Felicia whispered.

"She has? What is it this time?"

"She wants my address, and the addresses of the three children, as well as the painting of her mother and the Bible." And she held out the letter from the law firm.

"She has a lot of nerve," her husband said angrily after he had read it.

"I don't know. Don't you think maybe we should give her the things she's asking for? Livingston & Hill thinks so. After all, they do belong to her."

"Nonsense! She gave us all those things that were in storage."

"Carl, not the painting and the Bible. She just asked us to keep them for her."

"How is she going to prove that? We didn't sign any receipt for them. We're not a storage firm."

"No, but I *am* her cousin."

"So what? Do you realize that a painting by Shadrac was sold at auction in New York for over half a million dollars the other day? And that Bible is worth a good ten thousand—maybe more. Don't be foolish, Felicia!"

"Well, but it isn't as though we really needed the money."

"You don't, but what about me? Suppose something happens to you? I'm too old to get a job anymore."

"I'm afraid we may have trouble. Suppose she sues us?"

"She'd never win such a suit. Since she doesn't know where we live, she can't even have us served. Trust me, Felicia. I know what I'm doing."

"I'm sure you do, but I'm still worried. I don't want to get involved in a lawsuit."

"You won't be. She'll find herself stymied and after a while she'll go back to where she came from."

Felicia looked uncertain. "I know Hilary better than you do and she doesn't give up easily. She might succeed in getting in touch with the children."

"How is she going to do that? And what good will it do her if she does?"

"I suppose you're right."

"I'm going to start dinner. Shall I bring you a drink?"

"I don't believe I want one, thanks." Felicia still looked thoughtful and Carl looked at her speculatively.

"You sure? Come on, have one—it'll do you good."

"No, thank you, Carl."

"All right. You just rest. The paper has probably come; I'll bring it to you."

"All I ever do is rest," Felicia exclaimed petulantly. "I know you think doctors are all a lot of self-serving quacks out for a fast buck and that, left alone, the human body heals itself and I'm inclined to agree. But I'm getting awfully tired of this miserable life; I can't help wondering whether one of those diagnostic clinics—"

"We're not going into all that again! I won't allow you to be poisoned by medicines that corrupt the body. Believe me, nature's own remedies are the only effective ones. You admit yourself that you're much better this month than you were before."

"I'll admit I'm a little better than I was last month but then last month I was much worse than I was a few months earlier. My health seems to be on a sort of seesaw, going up and down, up and down." There was a lengthy pause. "You know," Felicia went on slowly, "perhaps it would be a good idea to see Hilary. After all, she is a nurse; she might be able to suggest something that would help me to get better. I wouldn't have to worry about her being out to make a quick buck. Returning her Bible and the portrait of her mother would be a cheap price to pay if she could help me get better."

"That's enough of that. Hilary Tarrant comes into this house over my dead body and I don't want any more argument from you about this. I just heard the gate bell ring; it's probably the paper, so I'll go get it for you," Carl said coldly.

The Dessein property was well protected. Surrounding it was a twenty-five-foot wall of reinforced concrete, spiked at the top, with pieces of jagged glass embedded between the spikes. Even the neighborhood cats knew better than to try to get into the garden. The gate itself could be opened only from within the house, and any prospective visitor, after stating his name and business into a two-way telephone system, was screened by closed-circuit television before the heavy iron gates swung open. For the past few years, however, there had been virtually no visitors. Newspapers, letters and small packages could be pushed through a large slot, which then locked itself.

Carl brought in the paper and handed it to Felicia, then went on into the kitchen to knead the bread and put it into pans for its second rising while he started dinner. Carl Dessein might have drawbacks as a husband but he was a superb domestic, worth his weight in gold, which was approximately what he succeeded in extracting from Felicia. She didn't realize it, but Walter Simmons' penchant for luxury cars cost her considerably less than Carl Dessein's penchant for cash.

Felicia opened the paper and began idly to turn the pages, but found it hard to take an interest in the news. Since she and Carl no longer went anywhere, she cared nothing for fashions, nor did the society pages hold her attention for long, though she liked occasionally to read about who, among her old friends' children, was marrying whom. She could hardly believe it when, one day, she read about the marriage of what turned out to be the granddaughter of one of her old schoolmates. She consoled herself with the recollection that this girl had been about four years her senior. Still, there was no getting around the fact that tempus was fugiting. She tossed the paper aside with a sigh of impatience. As it lay on the bolster at the other end of the sofa, her eye was caught by a boxed ad in the paper's personal column. "Will Felicia Dessein, née Wenham, formerly Mrs. Walter Simmons, or anyone having knowledge of her present whereabouts, please communicate with Julian Morel, Esq., at the 2214 Cordova Bank Building, Los Angeles, tel.: 627-5390 during office hours or with Hilary Tarrant (tel.: 942-1420 ext.

901) evenings and weekends." Felicia's eyes widened, her heart began to beat faster, and her hands became clammy. Suddenly and desperately, she longed to talk to Hilary. The problem was how to do it. Perhaps later on, if Carl went back into the garden after dinner? She was about to tear the ad out of the paper but realized that Carl would notice and not only ask what she had torn out but would buy another copy of the paper to check up on her. Felicia shivered as she remembered what had happened the last time she had disobeyed Carl. The trouble was that, since her illness, she was virtually a prisoner. "Not 'virtually.' I *am* a prisoner," she corrected herself, startled by the full realization of this fact. It had all come about so gradually and had seemed so inevitable.

The early years of Felicia's marriage to Carl had, in retrospect, been very satisfactory ones. After her divorce, she had felt overwhelmed by the responsibilities of raising three children. When she remarried, it had been wonderful to have Carl to turn to for advice and help, the children appeared to like him and her mother had thought her second marriage was a good one.

Hilary's visit had been the first cloud on the horizon; Carl disliked her violently, almost pathologically, and never missed an opportunity to make a derogatory remark about her whenever Mrs. McDougal or Nanny mentioned her; Felicia had learned never to do so.

Their first serious fight occurred when, going up to the attic one day, she found it virtually empty. Hilary's big Bible and the portrait of her mother were there, but all the other things that had belonged to her had disappeared while Felicia had been out of town attending the wedding of an old school friend.

"Where on earth are those things of Hilary's that were in the attic?" Felicia asked her husband.

"Those things weren't Hilary's, they belonged to us; I arranged to have them sold."

"But that's absurd, Carl. She didn't give us those things to sell; we said we wanted them to give the kids when they grew up."

"I didn't realize how valuable a lot of that stuff was—much too good for young people. I had an appraiser look it over and he said some of that furniture was Queen Anne and worth thousands. Keeping it would have meant increasing the insurance enormously so I decided to sell it. It brought in over sixty thousand dollars."

"Carl, that money belongs to Hilary! We'll have to send it to her."

"*You* can send it to her if you like," Carl shrugged. "I certainly don't intend to."

"What did you do with the money? Put it in our account?"

"Nope. I foresaw that you'd have the idiotic notion of sending it to her, so I put it in my own account."

"Carl, that's stealing; you're nothing but a common criminal!"

Felicia saw her husband's face turn white and she backed away from the expression of naked hatred on it.

"You're going to pay for that," he said between clenched teeth.

It came as something of a shock to Felicia when, lying across the bed sobbing into the pillow after her husband stormed out of the room, she realized that, in some strange way, she felt she deserved the beating Carl had administered.

Nothing more was said about the sixty thousand dollars.

Carl's stringent economizing began before they moved into the new house.

"The cost of living is zooming," Carl said one day, coming into Felicia's room with some bills in his hand. "You don't realize it because you don't handle our finances." This statement was true. In spite of her unfortunate experience with her first husband, she and Carl had a joint checking account and it was he who controlled it. Felicia rarely made out a check even for personal expenses. She merely told her husband when she needed money, which he at once provided, occasionally twitting her over her extravagance. As a matter of fact, Felicia was far from a spendthrift; like many wealthy women, she was almost parsimonious. But she had been taken aback when Carl suggested dismissing Hannah and Jake, the married couple who had worked for her for years.

"But why?" she had asked.

"You pay them an outrageously high salary, which they don't begin to earn. Then there's their keep and their Social Security. I'm sure, too, that Hannah gets a handsome kickback from the stores when she shops for food; that's why she was so angry when I decided to do the shopping myself."

"But what'll I do? I hate housework and I'm a lousy cook."

"I'll do the cooking and it'll be good for the children to do the cleaning and washing up and to work in the garden; the boys can certainly weed, mow the lawns and keep the hedges trimmed and I'll do the rest."

"Are you sure you want to do this?"

"I've got time on my hands since I don't go to work anymore. I'd enjoy it. Anyway, I keep telling you, our income doesn't buy as much as it did. We really need the money Hannah and Jake cost us."

Felicia sighed as she gave way.

It was after this that Felicia's marriage became very troubled. Meals became nightmares as Carl, no longer inhibited by the presence of a servant in the dining room, used this time for caustic diatribes, attacking the children for their various sins and misdemeanors; they, in turn, retreated into silence or impertinence and sometimes Felicia lay in bed at night and cried, wondering what she could have done to make God punish her so. Carl would put his arms around her and speak words of comfort, explaining that the children's behavior was not her fault but rather that of Walter Simmons' undoubtedly defective genes.

After Nanny Evans' departure, the children became even more obstreperous and difficult to manage. All three of them stayed out of the house as much as possible, spending as much time as possible at their friends' homes.

As they reached adolescence, the difficulties increased. Walter, the eldest, had been the first to cause serious problems. He turned rude, disrespectful, and ill-mannered, twice ran away from home, played hookey and finally took to staying out all night. When Felicia, following Carl's advice, punished him by stopping his pocket money, he helped himself from her purse and forged her signature on checks. It was Carl who had found the forged check in the boy's wallet before he had had a chance to cash it, who had put marked bills in Felicia's handbag when she began missing sizable sums and then found one of them in Timothy's pocket.

Nor were things easier with Jacqueline, who was disheveled and dirty, silent and sullen. When the final blow fell, it was Carl, tears running down his cheeks, who broke the news to her.

"My poor darling!" he said, putting his arms around his wife and holding her close.

"What's the matter?" Felicia exclaimed, alarmed. "What's happened?"

"I suppose it's partly my fault," he went on in a choked voice. "How could I possibly foresee it would be as bad as this. How could I know what Jacqueline would do?"

"What has she done? Quick, tell me!"

"She's been peddling dope in school."

"But how do you know?"

"I've suspected she was taking it for some time, so I hired a private detective. You can imagine how I felt when he reported that she was not only taking dope, but was a pusher."

"Oh, Carl! No! What'll we do?" she moaned.

"There's only one thing to do," Carl answered. "A school in Switzerland is the obvious answer."

So Jacqueline was bundled off to Switzerland.

Two years later, it was Timothy's turn. He began to duplicate the behavior of his older brother, with some new twists. By this time Felicia was too beaten down to do anything but agree with Carl that the only thing to do was to enroll him in a school well known for its stern discipline.

And that took care of Timothy.

In the days that followed the sudden, unexpected death of Mrs. McDougal, however, Carl proved a tower of strength. He relieved Felicia of the distressing task of making arrangements for the funeral and she was filled with gratitude. He had wanted to have the old lady cremated but Mrs. McDougal had left all instructions regarding her burial and had specifically stated she did not wish this to be done.

Carl had been surprised and disappointed when he learned that, while Felicia's income would increase, she would not receive all her mother's as a result of Mrs. McDougal's death.

After the fire which had destroyed their home, Felicia had bought a house not far from her mother's in Bel Air. With the children gone, it was too large for just the two of them, so Carl persuaded his wife to sell the place and let him build something more convenient on a one-acre lot near La Jolla he had found with a magnificent view of the sea. Felicia finally agreed and Carl designed and built the house they were now living in, much of it with his own hands. He wouldn't let her see it till it was completely finished and everything installed, down to the last saucepan. Following Mrs. McDougal's death, they had all her furniture, so Carl put a vast basement under the house in which they could store what they weren't actually using. But he never told Felicia, so she didn't know about the strong room concealed in the great central pillar which the house was built around; it contained the heating system, utilities, and plumbing in addition to the safe-room.

It turned out to be fortunate that they did move from the three-story house in Bel Air to the new place built on one floor in La Jolla. It was not long after they were settled in the new house that Felicia began feeling the first symptoms of the strange illness that crippled her and made stairs impossible for her to negotiate. It was almost as though Carl had precognition when he designed the new house, so carefully were all steps eliminated.

Felicia, hearing the whir of the meat grinder, picked up the newspaper again and studied Hilary's ad. The problem was how to answer it in view of Carl's opposition to any contact between them. There was no way of getting a letter out of the house without his knowledge, and the fact that she never knew how her voice was going to sound made telephoning a hazardous venture. But the more she thought about it the more she longed to see Hilary, convinced that her cousin, and perhaps only she, with her common sense and determination, was in a position to help her. Finally, her longing overcame her fear of Carl's anger. Committing Julian Morel's telephone number to memory, she got to her feet and, supporting herself with her walker, she made her way as quietly as she could to the telephone in the library, the farthest from the kitchen. With a shaking hand she dialed the lawyer's office, misdialed, and had to begin again. This time she got through but, in her nervous state, all that came out when she tried to talk was an almost inaudible whisper. Inaudible, that is, to the person at the other end of the line, who was firmly telling her to speak louder, but unfortunately all too audible to Carl, who had come noiselessly into the room and was staring at her with hate-filled eyes. He came slowly toward her as she tried to replace the receiver.

"So you did see that notice in the paper," he said. "And this is what you're up to after I forbade you to have anything to do with that bitch!" With precision, Carl slapped his wife as hard as he could four times, twice on each cheek.

"And if I catch you at the phone again, I'll take a whip to you, do you hear me?" And he strode out of the room, leaving Felicia scarlet-cheeked and sobbing. A moment later he went out the front door, a large knife in his hand. "Now you can't get any more ideas because I've cut the telephone wires," he announced when he returned. "Get to bed! You don't need any dinner!"

CHAPTER 17

Hilary and Julian Morel were in his office reminiscing as they sat hoping for a reply to their ad. When the phone rang, he was quick to answer it.

"I got someone on the line who's whispering and I can't hear who the caller wants to speak to. You said you were expecting an important call. You want me to put this through?"

"Yeah, put it through. This may be the call we're waiting for. You'd better take it," Julian said, holding out the receiver.

"Hello," Hilary said. "Is that you, 'Lisha?" She handed back the instrument. "All I heard was a sort of croaky whisper and then whoever it was hung up."

"Do you think it was your cousin?"

"I couldn't even make out if it was a man or a woman. If we don't get an answer to that ad, what shall we do next? Sue for the return of the Bible and the painting of Mother, as I suggested at our first meeting? As you said then, the trouble with lawsuits is that they take so long. I don't know why but I have an instinctive feeling that it's urgent to find Felicia—that she needs help. The feeling is even stronger now. That whispering voice was pretty unnerving."

"It's that damn law firm that blocks any normal approach. Even if we were to sue, it would be Livingston & Hill we'd have to serve," Julian said. "The addresses we've found, like for the car registration and the car insurance, are always Livingston & Hill—even the one on Carl Dessein's driver's license. By the way, I forgot to tell you that my informant in the Motor Vehicles Department told me that the driver's license in the name of Felicia Dessein, giving her old address, expired two years ago and hasn't been renewed."

"That's odd!" Hilary said with a frown. "Felicia loved to drive. She'd never have let her license expire. You know," she continued after a moment's thought, "those two couldn't have done a better job of covering any traces of their whereabouts if they had been criminals on the run. Could Felicia have died and Carl concealed her death so that the payments from the trust would continue?"

"That's pretty farfetched. I doubt if anything that melodramatic has happened. Anyway, Mr. Hill seems to be in constant communication with her. But she might be sick."

"Oh, I wish I hadn't allowed myself to be too angry with Felicia to come to California as soon as I heard about Aunt Louise's death. And there's something I haven't mentioned, Julian. *That* death was a little strange. Aunt Louise was an exceptionally healthy woman; I don't remember her ever having been ill, except for things like colds. And when I went to see Carrie she told me she hoped Felicia would arrange for an autopsy. Carrie said Aunt Louise had been for her annual checkup just a week earlier and the doctor said that she was healthier than most people thirty years younger. Is there any way we could have an autopsy done now?"

Julian shook his head.

"On what we have, we'd never get an exhumation order. Your aunt was elderly, after all, and old people do die unexpectedly sometimes."

"Perhaps the police would listen to us if we could link Aunt Louise's death with that of Abe Stein's mother. I told you Abie is *certain* Carl Dessein murdered her."

"You also told me there'd been an inquest and that the verdict was accidental death. It would be next to impossible to get that verdict overturned after all these years, particularly since the first Mrs. Dessein was cremated. No, what we have to do is continue to look for your cousin. Somebody who knows her should see our ad—her dentist, her hairdresser, her doctor, some friend."

There was a moment's silence.

"Say . . ."

"What . . ."

"I beg your pardon. What were you going to say?" Julian asked.

"I was going to say 'What fools we are.' We can get Felicia's address from Livingston & Hill, of course. All we have to do is to break in. I've been in that office heaps of times and it would be duck soup to burgle."

"I can't think why it's taken two well-trained, experienced former agents so long to think of something so obvious. If, between us, we can't pull off a simple little job like this—"

"Not 'we'; me. It would be ridiculous for you to get involved. If you got caught, you might well be disbarred; nothing much would happen to me. Even if my skills have become so rusty that I'm found out, Livingston & Hill would hardly press charges."

"Either I come along or it's no deal. I wouldn't miss the fun for anything."

"Okay. I'll go down and give the building the once-over: then, if we still don't have Felicia's address by this evening, we'll go and help ourselves to it."

"It's going to be a breeze," Hilary reported exuberantly later. "There's even an old-fashioned fire escape I'd never noticed before."

"I'm feeling young again," Julian answered. "I hope the phone doesn't ring, and do me out of my adventure. I'll meet you at the side door of your hotel at one-thirty A.M."

"Why the side door?"

"It seems more furtive."

They met with no problems, and when they got to their respective beds that morning, feeling thoroughly pleased with themselves, the two burglars had the information they wanted. Felicia's new home was in La Jolla.

CHAPTER 18

While it hadn't been easy to get hold of Felicia's address, Hilary was finding, now that she had it, that it was even harder to get hold of Felicia herself. The letters and telegrams she sent went unanswered and when she telephoned, she was first told the line was "out of order"; later this was changed to "disconnected." She then drove to the house, which stood on a little promontory just outside of La Jolla, but there was no response when she rang the bell at the heavy iron gate.

"You're wasting your time, lady. Those folks got closed television; they can see who's ringin' that bell and if they don't want to answer it, they don't. Seems like mostly they don't," a postman told her once when their visits coincided.

"Perhaps they're away."

"No indeedy, they're not away. They take in their mail regular, every day. The man who had this route before me said they don't never leave the house since the lady became a cripple."

"A cripple! What kind of a cripple?"

"I wouldn't know that, lady. Anyway, I ain't never seen her and I only seen him three or four times."

When Hilary returned to the hotel where she was staying, she telephoned Abe Stein to bring him up to date.

"It doesn't sound good," Abe said.

"It certainly doesn't. I'm determined to get into that house—and soon. If I can't get in any other way, I'll break in."

"I'll come with you," Abe said quickly.

"I wouldn't want you to do that. Where I'll need your help is in getting over the wall; my guess is that the damn thing is over twenty-five feet. It would take one hell of a ladder to get me over it, and I'd need help. And I wouldn't know how to get that long a ladder; a window-washing firm, perhaps?"

Abe thought for a moment.

"How about calling the fire department to report a fire at the Dessein place? Then, when the firemen force their way in, you could slip in after them."

"You haven't seen that gate. Even the fire department couldn't force its way in without smashing up their vehicles. If they rang the bell, Carl would simply tell them there was some mistake and that there was no fire. Of course, I'd be perfectly willing to set one but I'd have to be on the other side of the wall to do that. Any terrorist worth his salt knows how to get hold of a weapon that will cause a conflagration from a distance but unfortunately I don't. I'll have to use other weapons: bribery and corruption."

"Whom are you proposing to bribe and corrupt?"

"A fireman or two, from the hook-and-ladder truck . . . to get them to lend it to me. That wall would be no problem with a fire truck ladder."

"I doubt you'd find a fireman willing to take a chance. If he were found out, he'd be dismissed," Abe said slowly.

"I'd make it worth his while. You'd be surprised what people are willing to do for fifty thousand or so. I've had a lot of experience of bribery in my life."

"For that kind of money, you may be right. I hadn't realized you were thinking of going . . . Say, I believe I can help, after all!" Abe exclaimed. "I ran into a guy the other day who'd been in my outfit in Korea. In fact, he and I were among the few survivors of the prison camp we were in. So we had a couple of beers and brought each other up to date. He told me he'd made a career as a fireman here in L.A. He was planning to retire soon to open a little electrical repair store. I could try getting in touch with him. He likes to say I saved his life once, so he might listen to me. It wouldn't cost you fifty thousand dollars, either."

"I'll get off the line right now so that you can call him. And, for God's sake don't try to save me any money; he'll need quite a lot if he's planning to go into business for himself."

It took considerable eloquence on Abe's part to persuade Lew Trevelyan, his firefighting friend, to lend his assistance. In spite of Hilary's cynical assessment of mankind's frailty, instinct told Abe that this man wasn't bribable at any price. Instead, he told him the whole story, beginning with his own mother's probable murder.

"If it was anybody but you, my answer would be 'no way,'" Lew finally said. "However, since it is you . . . But I'm sure not going to let you have the truck. I'll drive it myself and I'll be in uniform. After all, I am the fire chief and I'll be able to think up a story if there are any questions."

"A kitten stuck in a tree?"

"I can do better'n that."

It was after ten o'clock that night that the fire engine, as silently as its powerful motor would permit, made its way along the rough, sandy road that skirted the wall around the back of the Dessein property. Hilary and Lew Trevelyan were alone in the truck, while Abe followed in his car. They had, in fact, had quite an argument before setting out.

"I'm coming with you and there's not going to be any argument about it; I wouldn't think of letting you tangle with that guy by yourself. Anyway, you seem to forget that I've got a stake in this, too," Abe had said before they set out.

Hilary finally capitulated.

"All right," she said. "But on one condition: that I break into the house alone. I can do it in complete silence. I was trained, if you want to know, and I don't want you spoiling things."

"We were taught to move quietly in Korea, too," Abe argued.

"That was years ago and I don't suppose you've been keeping in practice since you returned to civilian life."

"Have you?"

"Yep, I have. So now either you promise or we'll call the whole thing off and I'll find some other approach. Once I'm in, I'll let you know if I need help."

When the truck stopped and Hilary got off, Abe saw that she was dressed in a black leotard and black gloves, and wore black felt-soled shoes. She slipped a black stocking over her head and adjusted it so that the holes she had cut in it were over her eyes. Together she and Abe inspected the wall and selected a spot that was relatively free from tree branches at the point at which they would go over it. They went back to the truck and led Lew Trevelyan to the place they had chosen. The fire chief attached a heavy rope to the top rung of his ladder, which he let out till it was well above the wall, then adjusted it so that the rope hung free. Hilary climbed up the rungs of the ladder, transferred to the rope, then slowly let herself down. As soon as its lightness told Abe that Hilary had reached the ground, he followed her, albeit with more difficulty. Taking him by the hand, Hilary led him toward the lighted house. Suddenly she stopped and ducked behind a bush; her companion did the same. Silently they witnessed the scene before them.

For the past three days Felicia had been so frightened she hardly dared to allow herself to fall asleep. It was as though Carl had stripped a mask off his face and what was underneath was truly terrifying. Gone was any pretense of affection, of husbandly concern or even of ordinary humanity. She had accustomed herself to her husband's occasional outbursts of anger and to his blows whenever she crossed him in any way. But the way he was behaving now was different—quite different. For three days now Carl had kept her locked up in her bedroom, sometimes neglecting even to bring her meals.

"Please let me out," Felicia had quavered the second time this had happened. "I can manage for myself if you'll only let me out. I haven't done anything to you."

"You're a two-faced, conniving bitch. I caught you trying to get your cousin here and you know how I feel about her."

"But, Carl, I thought perhaps she could help me to get better. I'm tired of being sick and helpless all the time—of being such a burden on you."

"You won't be a burden on me much longer," Carl Dessein answered with an ugly laugh. The next day the only food he brought her was a loaf of bread, and he completely ignored the repeated ringing of her bell. He spent most of his time in his strong room, sorting papers and packing them and various packets into a valise which he had at his feet. It was nearly eleven when he closed and locked the valise, glanced at his watch and went into his wife's room. He found her sitting by the window sobbing.

"Oh, shut up and get to bed," he ordered roughly, coming toward her. "You don't have to act like that; I'm not going to hurt you," he added as she shrank away from him, her arm upraised as if to ward off a blow. "Just get to bed."

"I'm hungry, I want some dinner—I don't want to go to bed."

"I don't care what you want." Picking Felicia up, he carried her across the room and threw her on the bed.

"At least let me go to the bathroom; I haven't washed."

"You can go to bed dirty tonight," Carl answered. From the pocket of the gold-embroidered red velvet dressing gown he was wearing he took out several lengths of nylon cord.

"Carl, what are you going to do? No!" Felicia screamed.

"I'm not going to strangle you, if that's what you're worried about. I've got a lot to do tonight and I want to make sure I'm not bothered."

"How can I bother you when you lock me in here?"

"This is to make doubly sure." And Carl proceeded to attach his wife's arms and legs to her bed, paying no attention to her cries of protest.

"When will you unloose me?" Felicia called despairingly as he moved to the door.

"When I get around to it," he answered; he turned off the light, left the room and locked the door behind him.

Hilary and Abe Stein stood outside the window in the shadows and watched the scene.

"I'm going in now through the living room," she murmured to her companion, leading the way. Except for a dim light in one corner, the room was in darkness. Hilary draped a black sash around her neck. She then undid a bag that hung from her waist and took out material which she quickly taped to the window; as deftly as any burglar she proceeded to use a cutter and the glass fell noiselessly against the taped-on material. Abe took it from her hand and carefully stood it against the wall while Hilary turned to go through the opening she had made. "Wait for the signal," she mouthed to Abe as she entered the house.

Once she was in, Hilary stood still for a few moments to allow her eyes to get used to the near-darkness, then cautiously made her way toward the only room in which she could see a light. Silently she approached the open door and looked in; it proved to be the kitchen but it was empty. Hilary was puzzled; surely Carl would not be sitting in one of the darkened rooms. Assuming that he would soon make an appearance, Hilary flattened herself against the wall and waited. The minutes dragged by interminably and she became seriously concerned, fearing that Abe would worry about her prolonged absence and jump the gun. Suddenly, to her astonishment, a wall slid open and Carl, struggling to lift a heavy suitcase across a raised sill, appeared in the kitchen. Hilary removed the black stocking covering her face and stepped forward.

"Carl!" she said.

The man, twirling around, gave an unearthly yell as he dropped the suitcase. For a moment he stared at her unbelievingly.

"You!" he exclaimed. He ran back the way he had come and returned with a gun in his hand. Not waiting to take aim, he fired. Hilary had already covered her head with the scarf around her neck when she felt a searing pain as the bullet grazed her shoulder. She pulled the plastic weapon out of her pocket and, aiming it in Carl's direction, pushed the button to release the poison and ran as fast as she could, colliding with Abe.

"Don't go in there!" she said urgently. "It isn't safe."

"Where is he?"

Hilary didn't answer but stood clutching Abe, listening. Finally she heard a dull thud.

"Where is Carl?" Abe repeated.

"Probably in hell," Hilary finally answered. "No, don't go in there yet," she went on. "There's nothing more to be done about Carl. Let's go to Felicia."

"Did you shoot him?" Abe asked anxiously.

Hilary put her hand to her shoulder and felt the stickiness of wet blood.

"No, he shot me," she answered as she returned her weapon to her pocket.

CHAPTER 19

To say that Felicia's late husband was a murderous lunatic is, I fear, too kind [Hilary wrote, nearing the end of a long letter to Ian]. I don't believe he was a lunatic at all. He would have murdered his wife years ago had it not been for the terms of the Kincaid trust. Since he couldn't inherit from Felicia, it was to his advantage to keep her alive while he built up capital for himself out of what he could save from her income—and there he certainly did a great job.

After he had forced the children away from home, Carl and Felicia pretty much led the life of recluses, spending less than fifty per cent of her income. The strong room he had built turned out to contain about $200,000 in cash as well as stock certificates (in his name), silver and gold bars and several bags of loose gems and other valuables, including the jewelry I had given to the children, and, of all things, my Shadrac portrait of Mother, the Tarrant family Bible and my silver. All of this, at a first rough estimate, amounts to more than a million dollars. It seems to me beautifully ironic that all this wealth, which Carl worked so hard to extract from Felicia, goes back to her as his widow, since he died intestate.

Felicia will recover, though it's taken awhile to

find out just what's wrong with her. She told us that she suffered from frequent attacks of nausea and a gradual weakening of her muscles. When the doctors first examined her after Carl's death they thought she had had a stroke, but after she had been in the hospital for a few days, she began to get better at a fairly rapid clip.

Neither Abe Stein nor I have any doubt but that Carl was responsible for the sudden death of Aunt Louise as well as that of his mother. But there's no point in bringing either of these murders up now, since Carl is dead.

Felicia told us that she had periods of feeling quite well but that these were invariably followed by a relapse. That devil had been systematically feeding her a combination of venomous plants—*veratrum*, which induces vomiting, muscular weakness, difficulty in walking and, later, a general paralysis, and *zigadenus*, known as "death comas," which produces much the same symptoms. The advantage of the latter is that this plant retains its poisonous properties even when dried, which permits its use in seasons when the fresh plants are unobtainable. Both grow readily in the West and, in fact, we found carefully tended patches of both veratrum and zigadenus in a corner of the garden, as well as a large jar of dried zigadenus in the kitchen. Carl was careful to give her only enough to incapacitate her, not to kill her. But every time she seemed to be recovering, he had to give her a new dose.

Fortunately, no one had the least suspicion that

Carl died of anything other than heart failure—which, of course, he did. We worked very fast after we were sure Carl was dead. Felicia was unconscious and we had to cut through the rope with which he had tied her up. I had no heart stimulant handy but got her to swallow some very strong tea, which worked. I then cleaned her up and Abe and I carried her to Carl's room where we put her in bed. She knew me and clutched my hand, trying to talk, but I couldn't understand what she was saying.

Then Abe succeeded in unlocking the very tricky front gate, he and his fireman friend quickly and quietly took down the ladder which I had used to get over the wall, and drove the truck away. It was only after they had gone that I changed into some clothes of Felicia's and called for help.

I am reasonably sure that no one suspects me of being responsible for Carl's death. My story was quite straightforward: Felicia had written me that she was ill and I, a nurse, had come to take care of her, arriving two days earlier. In the course of the night I had heard a noise and had found Carl lying on the floor. Since I was unable to detect a heartbeat, I had called 911 to ask for emergency aid.

Felicia is out of the hospital now and I'm taking her to Acapulco to convalesce. As a surprise for her, I've arranged to have all three children meet us there. I asked her yesterday how she had borne being separated from them and she said that sometimes, in the night, her longing for them amounted to physical pain but that the relief of no longer having to go through the terrible daily scenes almost compensated for their absence. She didn't answer when I asked why she hadn't abandoned her husband and stayed with the children.

So that's an account of my doings since I saw you last and I now realize I am definitely too old for such fun and games. The fact that I am responsible for the death of yet another fellow being isn't bothering me unduly this time. Somehow I can't think of Carl Dessein as a "fellow being"—he was more like a vicious animal. What I did was in self-defense; he would certainly have killed Felicia and me had I not got him first. So it has all worked out and I am more grateful than I can say for that strike in Paris which left me in possession of your "weapon." But I can hardly wait to get it back into your hands now.

I'll call you as soon as I know just when I'm coming back to England. Very soon, I hope.

All my love, darling.

Hilary

Nearly a month later Ian received a cable from Hilary. "How would you like to marry me quickly," he read. "Felicia is planning to wrap those tendrils of her around me and I can't face it. Save me!"

"Arriving Tuesday. Get license soonest," Ian cabled back.

Alexandra Roudybush has received wide acclaim and a growing following for her novels of suspense and intrigue: *Female of the Species*, *A Gastronomic Murder*, *A Sybaritic Death*, *The House of the Cat*, and *Suddenly, in Paris*. She is an American who has lived, quite literally, all over the world. Her father was a foreign newspaper correspondent, and her husband, now retired, was in the diplomatic service. She now lives in Aveyron, France.